T0368319

# POLLUTED HEART

Love will destroy what it cannot fix

by
Khari D. Akpan

Inspired by a true story

authorHOUSE®

*AuthorHouse™*
*1663 Liberty Drive*
*Bloomington, IN 47403*
*www.authorhouse.com*
*Phone: 1-800-839-8640*

*© 2011 Khari D. Akpan. All rights reserved.*

*No part of this book may be reproduced, stored in a retrieval system,*
*or transmitted by any means without the written permission of the author.*

*First published by AuthorHouse    9/04/2009*

*ISBN: 978-1-4389-2655-1 (sc)*

*Printed in the United States of America*
*Bloomington, Indiana*

*This book is printed on acid-free paper.*

# POLLUTED HEART

Love will destroy what it cannot fix

# POLLUTED HEART

## PLOT SUMMARY

**Genres:** Drama

**Tagline:** Love will destroy what it cannot fix.

**Plot Outline:** A man's life begins to unravel when he finds himself fighting between moral obligation to his family and emotional commitment to his lover.

**Plot Synopsis:** Chad and Lana Miller appear to live a happy life, raising four children in a fine neighborhood, but Chad is slipping deeper and deeper into a secret affair with Erica Lake, who is oblivious to his marriage.

Although it confronts racial tension, Polluted Heart is a captivating story about relationships that bluntly attacks today's realities on the strangest passion the world has ever known -- Love!

**High Concept:** "CRASH" meets "American Beauty." People of varied circumstance collide in one crisis -- love treated unfairly.

## Treatment

For **CHAD MILLER**, extra-marital affairs with **JANICE MARSH** is nothing more than a frolicsome escapade, but his secret union with Case Manager **ERICA LAKE**, who's oblivious to his marriage, is spinning his life out of control.

Her intelligence, her beauty, and her ability to love and nurture him just the right way, captivate Chad's heart and mind like no other, ever could.

However, Chad has his lovely wife **LANA**, and four wonderful children. Morally, Chad knows that his newfound love is in the way of his family. But emotionally, he feels that his family is in the way of his newfound love.

His goal isn't to hurt his family or to chalk up women like points on a scoring card, but Chad is compelled above sensual weakness… beyond sexual need… in his thirst for women lie something darker… something deeper.

Seeking answers from **DR. SEAN LEVIN**, a philosophical sex therapist, Chad completely opens up, telling his embarrassing distress of feeling sexually inadequate, and his discomforting childhood fears of being immortalized with the crown, "Fag," like that of his father.

Dr. Levin discovers that Chad's obsession with women is really an obsession with distinguishing himself from his dad, and validating his manhood, despite his phobia of sexual inadequacy.

Chad's obstructing issues and serious childhood marks of shame interfere with his emotional intelligence toward women, and life in general.

Balancing home and a secret love affair becomes too big a juggling act for Chad. Unable to give enough to either situation has created a dismal world for him.

Chad knows his dishonest lifestyle can't go on, and although he hasn't been brave enough to reveal his disgraceful and brutal truths of betrayal and deception, Lana and Erica are sensing levels of deceit in the man they both love.

The pressure of being discovered strain Chad's mental and emotional health beyond repair, and becomes unhinged.

It's all on the line now -- his affair, his marriage, his family, his aspirations, his sanity, and his very existence.

# WISH LIST

**ERICA**................. Taraji P. Henson (Alt. Jennifer Hudson)

**CHAD**................. Terrence Howard

**LANA**................. Alfre Woodard

**ROSINA**.............. Loretta Divine

**JAMES**................ Samuel L. Jackson

**LISA**................ Keke Palmer

**DRAKE**............... John Witherspoon

**MRS. LUCY**........... BeBe Drake

## **DEDICATED**

To Suzanne L. Dandie, Desiree L. Wilkins, Diamond S. Wilkins, Shalik J. Young, Khari E. Z. Wilkins, and Khavon G. D. Wilkins. Suzanne, Thank you for all of your love and support during the development of this story. And to my children, thank you for bearing with dad in his absence while working hard to develop and write this story. I love you all so much! You are all greatly appreciated.

**OPENING SCENES:**

**CHAD MILLER**, late twenties with an athletic build and his
ball cap flipped backwards. He's at the desktop putting the
finishing touches on his screenplay.

His good-looking wife, **LANA** passes in the BACKGROUND,
carrying two-year-old **CHAD JR** on her hip.

Chad collects the final pages from the printer. He evens out
the manuscript so that the three-hole-punches are lined
perfectly.

He binds the manuscript with gold brads... kisses Lana and
the baby on the cheek... Chad hugs and kisses each of his
three daughters, **JOY** 12, **SABRINA** 10, and **DIANA** 9... Chad is
out the front door, manuscript cuffed in hand.

Chad hops into a prehistoric mail jeep. After several
attempts the dilapidated vehicle finally ignites.

Chad hurries through a pair of automatic doors in a lavish
office building.

Chad exits the elevator... he steps through an office with a
smile... drops his manuscript entitled, **"PERFECT FIT,"** on the
desk.

Chad places a USB stick atop the manuscript and stands self-
confident.

A beautiful literary agent, named **SHELLY DAID** smiles back and
gives a victorious fist-pump.

Shelly grabs the USB stick. She uploads an electronic copy of
the screenplay.

WE'RE LOOKING OVER HER SHOULDER when she keys the email
account, **caregroup@s.Levin.net**

**SEAN GOLDBERG**, early 40's wearing a stylish suit and chatting
on his cellular, opens an email message from Shelly Daid.

We look over Sean's shoulder and the title page of Chad's
script fill the screen. Sean shifts his mouse and clicks the
print command.

                    CHAD (VOICE OVER)
          Finally, I was satisfied with the
          conclusion of my script. My dream
          is to become a Hollywood green-
          lighter.
                    (MORE)

                    CHAD (VOICE OVER) (cont'd)
          My representative, Shelly, she's
          looking to establish herself as a
          top agent. She has this connection
          with an extremely wealthy Doctor of
          some sort, whose looking to break
          into the Hollywood scene as an
          Exec. So, Shelly thought that my
          script could be the vehicle to help
          us all reach our goals.


**FADE IN:**


**EXT. URBAN AMERICA - CRIME DISTRICT - DAY**

The violent, drug-infested neighborhood is in full swing.
Sounds of urban America assault our ears.

The THUNDER of chopper blades WHIPPING through the sky,
WAILING police sirens in the distance. A BLARING ambulance
somewhere nearby.

The open window of some run-down house is PUMPING out a Lil'
Wayne hit.

Thuggish teens roam about. The butt of a handgun peek from
one teen's jacket.

Another teen stashes a high-powered assault rifle in an alley
dumpster.

Two other teens rush a car and battle for a dope sale. A
brief argument erupts before one teen draws an automatic
weapon. The other backs off.

Chad's fuddy-duddy Jeep pulls into our view. It slows and
stop at the red light. The engine sputters and coughs, then
chokes completely and shuts down.


**INT. JEEP - DAY**

Chad is frustrated with his piece-of-shit jeep. He pumps the
gas and turns the ignition again and again. The engine
heaves, desperate to start, but doesn't quite turn over.

Chad stares at us through his rear view mirror. His eyes bug
with sudden awe. He turns to look over his shoulder.

**EXT. STREET - DAY**

A 2009 Audi R8 pulls behind Chad. It's silver with a showroom gloss and a gleaming, chrome grill. It's the epitome of grace and style.

The thuggish teens also admire the Audi from their post.

**INT. AUDI - DAY**

The driver is Sean Levin, and again, he is busy on his cellular.

As Sean listens to the chatting voice over the phone, he tucks the screenplay, "Perfect Fit" into his expensive satchel.

>                    SEAN
>           (to phone)
>      Yes, I've read the script, and I
>      love it.
>           (beat)
>      Powerful story! Maybe think about
>      giving the character "Dario" a
>      stronger name.

**INT. SHELLY'S OFFICE - DAY**

Shelly does a victory dance in her swivel chair and flashes a broad smile.

>                    SHELLY
>           (to phone)
>      Sean, baby, this can be what we've
>      all been dreaming of.
>           (beat)
>      Yeah! They've signed the letter of
>      intent. They're sitting right here
>      in front of me.

Shelly give a thumbs-up to Mos Def and Meagan Goode, whom are lounging across from her.

**INT. ADUI - DAY**

Sean appears distracted. Suddenly, he realizes he's on the wrong street.

Sean watches nervously over each shoulder, looking for signs of trouble from the hoodlums. He power-locks the car doors.

                    SEAN
               (to phone)
          Shelly, your word is gold with me.
          If you say a flea can pull the
          load, then damnit, hitch the load
          to the flea.
               (laughs; looks around)
          Yeah. Look. I gotta hang up. Turned
          down the wrong block. Central
          Avenue. Not the route I like
          driving home. I'd rather go down,
          up, and around.
               (beat; to phone)
          Yea! Exactly. Out of my habitat.
          Definitely on the wrong side of the
          economic divide.
               (beat)
          Ok sweetie.

Sean flips the phone closed and drops it in his chest pocket.
The traffic light flashes green.

Sean is anxious to move, but he can see Chad struggling to
crank his jeep.

A car BLARING obnoxious rap music pulls behind Sean, and
makes him feel boxed in, like a sitting duck.

Sean HONKS his horn frantically! He is desperate for the jeep
to drive off, but the old contraption remains stuck.

Sean's neck moves this way and that. His face flushes with
fear and worry.

                    SEAN
               (sotto)
          Theses bastards are trying to car-
          jack me. What bullshit!

Sean looks left, and out of nowhere, a thug approaches. He's
staring, treasuring, and worshipping the Audi.

The thug peers in the driver window and is fascinated by the
digital gauge cluster.

Sean can't take the pressure. He jerks the steering wheel and
pins the gas, determined to get around the jeep and not
caring if he runs down the thug doting over his ride.

Sean pulls alongside the jeep and powers down the passenger
window.

Chad looks over. His face apologetic for the delay.

Sean glares at Chad as if he's beneath minimal standards of human decency, and he flips Chad the bird.

                    SEAN
              (speeding off)
          Not to day, buddy. Fuck you!


**INT. JEEP - DAY**

Chad stares coldly, furious with the insult. He turns the ignition angrily, and pumps the gas pedal, raging for the engine to crank. And finally, it ignites -- VROOM, VROOOOOM!

The Audi's blinker flashes several blocks up. Chad pins the gas, and merely beats the yellow light in his brazen chase for the Audi.

Chad zips up the street at psychotic speed. The environment changes from seedy, ill-kept apartment buildings to newly-built high-rises, clearly showing an economic divide in the community.


**EXT. HIGH-RISE COMPLEX - PARKING LOT - DAY**

Sean exits the Audi carrying his pricey leather satchel. His posture weak and flimsy. And he's is still shaken-up by the idea of being trapped at the light.

A Ferrari Spyder pulls up to the security arm. The woman driving smiles at the young guard manning the security house, then She swipes her key-pass. The security arm rears.

Then, without warning, a high-reving engine DRONES very nearby. The startled woman cranes her neck to see what's the commotion.

But before she can figure out what's going on, Chad's noisy jeep maneuvers around her with SQUEALING tires.

Chad SCREECHES to a halt and SWERVES into an odd parking angle. He steps out the jeep and SLAMS the door shut.

Sean attempts to duck between two luxury cars, but realizes he's already been noticed and decides against it.

There's no hiding the horror on Sean's face as he fidgets with his satchel.

Chad gaits closer. His construction boots loosely laced and open at the top.

The rugged boot-soles SPLASH through a pool of water. Chad's fists ball tightly and his face screws with intense displeasure.

Some curious residents peer from their terrace. Others from the parking lot.

A nervous woman, cupping a Shih zu in her arms, scrambles through her purse. She retrieves her cell phone and punches numbers frantically.

Sean fumbles through his pockets and take out his wallet, some loose cash, and his titanium phone.

When Chad reaches him, Sean extend his personals nervously to this angry stranger.

                    SEAN
          Here... take it all. Just don't
          shoot!

Chad is becomes more offended. He SLAP the personals violently from Sean's hand.

The titanium phone splits open on IMPACT and fragments buckshot from the ground.

Chad drills Sean with an icy glare. His angry breath huffing in Sean's frightened face.

                    CHAD
          Do you see a gun?!

                    SEAN
          No. Thankfully, I don't.

                    CHAD
          Sorry to disappoint you, but I'm
          not here to rip you off.
               (off Sean's look)
          Were you looking for a fight? Is
          that why you flipped me off?

                    SEAN
               (terrified; steps back)
          Look, I had a really bad day.

                    CHAD
          A really bad day?! Is that all?
          Cause, I had a really bad <u>life</u>!

                        SEAN
          Your bad life is no fault of mine,
          right?

                        CHAD
          And your bad day is no fault of
          mine.
               (leans in)
          So don't punish me for it with your
          rude gestures, you got it.
               (angrier)
          Don't you ever disrespect me!

Sean's satchel slips from his hand and THUDS the ground. Chad
seems to gain some satisfaction from Sean's apparent fear.

                        CHAD
          Pick up your things and get out my
          face.

Sean keeps a wary gaze on Chad, this furious stranger to him,
as he stoops to retrieve his satchel and personals.

Sean can see Chad's fury mounting as he gathers his things.

                        CHAD
          You piece of shit!

                        SEAN
               (his voice breaks)
          Now there's a contradiction. You
          say don't ever disrespect you. An-
          and you call me a "Piece of shit."

Chad's angry face changes to one of oddity. Sean has a valid
point and Chad knows it.

In an effort of restrain, Chad sucks wind and blows it out
through puffed cheeks, then he turns to walk away.

Sean is relieved to see Chad going, but Chad stops after only
two steps, then whirls with his right arm.

Tension cannot hide from Sean's face. He flinches in fear of
a possible blow.

But Chad is only offering a friendly hand. Chad's face
appears overcome by logic and rational. He seems to have
reached a mental calm.

Sean is stumped by the gesture. He stares for an
uncomfortable beat.

                    CHAD
                (hand extended)
            You're right. You're absolutely
            right. I'm sorry for the way I
            spoke to you.

Sean cautiously extends his hand as well. They shake. An
eerie shake at first. Sean's eyes watch Chad carefully. He
sees the peace and tranquility underneath Chad's anger.

Sean clutches more firmly and shakes with greater confidence.
Then they release. Chad turns and walks away, again.

Sean takes a moment to process what just went down. He
strokes his hair with his hand as he watches Chad's back.

The nervous woman scuttles to a squad car. Her pointing
finger jumps from Chad to Sean. Her mannerisms more fierce
when pointing to Chad.

The officer realizes peace has been made. He gestures the
woman to relax.

                    SEAN
            Hey. Buddy.

Chad turns.

                    SEAN
            I don't know what to say. Hadn't
            considered real engine trouble.
            Thought you seemingly broke down,
            and that you guys were setting the
            stage on me. I'm sorry if that's
            stereotypical. But I had a
            legitimate fear for my life. When I
            thought I beat the odds, I kind of
            gave you a rude "Ah-ha."


TIGHT ON CHAD

                    CHAD
            forget about it.


**INT. COFFEE SHOP - STILL TIGHT ON CHAD - MORNING**

PULL BACK to reveal Chad at a window side table with **ERICA
LAKE,** an attractive care manager in her early thirties.

Erica's face transits from horror to relief as she CLINKS her
coffee mug to the saucer softly.

                    ERICA
I'm just so thankful you didn't
fight the man.

                    CHAD
          (sips coffee)
I don't know if that makes me
prejudice, crazy, or what? Think I
need to see someone --
professional?


                    ERICA
It wouldn't hurt. But, were you
okay with that?  That resolution?

                    CHAD
Initially, I felt that he flipped
me with racial abuse.

                    ERICA
What changed your perspective?

                    CHAD
Thinking twice about it. Maybe he
just flipped me out of impatience,
or whatever. Maybe he *didn't* flip
because I was black. But maybe I
took it way too personal because he
was *white*.

                    ERICA
Well, it is awfully mature of you
to hold yourself accountable.

                    CHAD
I just wasn't sure if my anger
actually brewed because of his
prejudice, or my own.
          (beat)
So, yeah. I was okay with that
resolution.

                    ERICA
Good. Then your reaction doesn't
make you neurotic, or prejudice.

                    CHAD
I shouldn't let myself get so
worked-up over nothing, though.

                    ERICA
Relax, Sweetie. Your reaction just
shows the human side of you.
                    (MORE)

                    ERICA (cont'd)
And your *resolve*, it shows the wise
and mature side of you.


                    CHAD
You always have the right things to
say.


                    ERICA
The truth is easy to explain. And
now he knows that not every black
man with his hat on backwards is
crazy and deranged.

Chad appreciates her perspective.


**EXT. COFFEE SHOP - MORNING**

Chad and Erica emerge onto the sidewalk through the shop's
double doors.

They weave through the busy downtown crowd with their hands
interlocked.

                    ERICA
               (smiling)
I feel like you're growing up right
before my eyes.


                    CHAD
Old friends say I'm not the same
dude. But they think I squared up
instead of grown up. I don't know
what they expect from me.


                    ERICA
               (repulsed)
Forget what they expect.
               (beat; calmer)
Your behavior is changing. You're a
man now. A grown ass man. And you
don't need to be identified as some
mythical figure for shit you did as
a boy.

They finally reach Erica's Sedan. She peeks at her watch and
realizes she's running late. She kisses his cheek quickly.

                    ERICA
Omigosh! I have a twelve-O'clock.
Then, gotta be in court. But have
to stop at the office first. I'm
free after that. See you later?

                    CHAD
          later sounds good.

                    ERICA
               (happy)
          Can't wait!

                    CHAD
          I'll be shooting some pool around
          three. Pick me up me at the bar.


                    ERICA
               (as she gets in the car)
          And look for a job!

## INT. ERICA'S SEDAN - NEW YORK, NY - DAY

Erica parks in front of Hunter University, which sits in the heart of the city.

She hugs the steering wheel and takes a deep breath. She's all keyed about something.


## EXT. HUNTER UNIVERSITY - NY, NY - DAY

Erica pulls her receipt from the meter. She places it on the dashboard so that it is visible to parking enforcement officers.

## INT. GUIDANCE COUNSELOR'S OFFICE - MORNING

Erica sits across from PROFESSOR BARNES. Her eyes glossy and her shoulders slumped in defeat. The old, studious gentleman looks empathetic.


                    ERICA
          I don't want to deny the promotion.
          That's just poor work ethic. But if
          I accept it. Formality is, they
          investigate my academic records.
          Then, they learn that I don't
          actually have my master's yet.

                    PROFESSOR BARNES
          I truly understand my dear. But
          it's not a decision I have the
          power to make.

                    ERICA
               (pleading)
     But you do have the power,
     Professor. If you truly understand,
     then convince the board that this
     student... this woman... this
     mother, deserves a chance. Please.
     I just need one semester. Only
     eight credits more?

                    PROFESSOR BARNES
     It is really out of my hands.
               (passes her a form)
     Complete this form of academic
     forgiveness, and plead your case.

                    ERICA
     What are my chances?

                    PROFESSOR BARNES
     Well. Your reasons for withdrawal
     are highly acceptable to the mind.
     That makes your chances better than
     mediocre. However, it has been over
     five years. That makes your chances
     less than excellent. Nonetheless,
     There's nothing to lose.

Erica accepts the form with very little faith.


## EXT. NYC - MEAT PACKING DISTRICT - DAY

We follow a well-dressed Chad across the busy loading docks
and into the meat storehouse.


## INT. MEAT STOREHOUSE - RECEPTIONIST DESK - DAY

Chad approaches LIZ the receptionist.

                    CHAD
     Good morning. Chad Miller. I have a
     1 PM interview.

                    LIZ
     Have you filled out an application?

                    CHAD
     No, ma'am.

She hands him a clipboard and application. He goes for an ink
pen from his chest pocket.

Chad takes a seat and sift through the papers. There's an aptitude test on grammar and math attached, but that's not what shakes him.

CLOSE ON APPLICATION

**Have you ever been convicted of a felony? If yes, explain here** _____.

Dejection sweeps his face. He flips the application back to the front page. Reluctantly, he begins filling it out.

He returns the application and clipboard to Liz. She reviews it rather quickly. Before Chad could step away-

>                     LIZ
>           List your references please. Even
>           if you have it with your resume.
>           And you didn't give your salary
>           requirements.

As he retakes the clipboard a short man in khakis and a plaid shirt walks up. He's 50ish with large square frames and graying hair. He's the storehouse manager, PHIL KEARST.

>                     LIZ
>           Morning, Phil.

>                     PHIL
>           How are ya' Liz?

>                     LIZ
>           Another day in paradise.

>                     PHIL
>           Eh, the day just started. Give it
>           some time.
>                (to Chad)
>           Chad Miller?

>                     CHAD
>           Yes, sir.

They shake.

>                     PHIL
>           Hi, Phil Kearst. Follow me.

**INT. EMPLOYEE CAFETERIA - DAY**

It's clean and unoccupied. Phil and Chad enter through the
SQUEAKY swinging doors. Phil stares for a beat, unsure where
to sit.

> PHIL
> Aw hell. I guess this is fine.
> (to Chad)
> If you could just pull up a chair
> from right there.

> CHAD
> (as he sits)
> Thank you for this opportunity, Mr.
> Kearst.

> PHIL
> (views application;sotto)
> Came here through a staffing
> agency. Aced the aptitude test.
> (beat)
> Hm. sketchy work history here.
> Haven't worked much, huh.

As he continues through the application Chad looks nervous.

> PHIL
> I see. You have a criminal
> background. Aggravated assault,
> Possession of a firearm, and...
> what is cds?

> CHAD
> Controlled dangerous substance.

> PHIL
> (shocked)
> Jeez! Like an explosive?

> CHAD
> No, sir. Like illegal drugs.

> PHIL
> (embarrassed)
> Well, in this age of terror attacks
> you can see how that acronym and
> definition may confuse some.

> CHAD
> Sure.

                    PHIL
          Hm. Did you seek help?

                    CHAD
               (confused)
          Excuse me?

                    PHIL
          Are you rehabilitated?

                    CHAD
          Oh, no, sir.
               (off Phil's look)
          I mean, I wasn't a user. I,
          unfortunately, was a dealer.

                    PHIL
          Well, you're smart not to lie,
          'cause we background check. Is the
          huge gap of unemployment due to an
          ultimate incarceration?

                    CHAD
          It is.

                    PHIL
          How long were you in for?

                    CHAD
          Too long.

                    PHIL
          Guess it made a man outta' ya?

                    CHAD
          Actually, it didn't. It made a fool
          out of me. What makes a man out of
          a boy is not surviving a prison
          term. But instead, being able to
          flourish in the free world.

                    PHIL
          Hm. That's pretty poetic. And I'm
          sure you mean something by that. I
          just don't know what.

Phil tries to look as normal as possible, but clearly bias
has set in.

                    PHIL
          Well, we're going to be
          interviewing for the next few
          weeks.
                    (MORE)

                    PHIL (cont'd)
The position we're trying to fill
is a small one, but vital to our
daily operation, so I hope you can
understand why it's important for
us to choose the right guy. After
we're done interviewing, the
director and myself will make a
collective decision on are man.
Fair enough?

                    CHAD
          (crestfallen)
Fair enough. Thank you again, for
the opportunity.

They shake. Chad walks away. Phil peeks at the application
again. He turns and looks up, almost like he wants to call
Chad back and give him a chance.

But instead, he only watches with sympathy as Chad pushes
through the SQUEAKY swinging doors and out of sight.


**EXT. NYC BUSINESS DISTRICT - DAY**

Erica hustles through the revolving doors of a ritzy office
building.


**INT. BOARD ROOM - DAY**

Erica's late for a staff meeting which is already in progress
with her EXECUTIVE DIRECTOR and a team of SOCIAL SERVICE
WORKERS.

She mouths "Hello" to TONY, a handsome colleague, as she
sits. He nods.

                    CASE MANAGER
I just don't know what to do. His
wife is our client, not him.

                    ERICA
Is this the Dorrity case?

                    PROGRAM COORDINATOR
Yes.

                    ERICA
You should still council him. Not
in a clinical sense because we
can't bill him.
                    (MORE)

                    ERICA (cont'd)
But just have a discussion with him
regarding what his day is like and
who oversees his wife while he's
gone.

                    PROGRAM AIDE
          (to exec. Director)
Are Alzheimer clients billed
differently than psychiatric
service clients?

                    PROGRAM AIDE #2
Offhand I'm not sure, but I think
so.

                    EXECUTIVE DIRECTOR
No offhand information unless it's
100 percent accurate. We have an
obligation to verify.


                    ERICA
Yes, they are billed differently.

                    EXECUTIVE DIRECTOR
There's your answer.

                    PROGRAM AIDE #1
You sure?

                    ERICA
Absolutely. It only makes sense.

                    TONY
We have too many open cases. Cases
of clients whom we no longer have
contact with.

                    ERICA
Confusion is the recurring theme.
It seems are system is not in
place. The structure is beginning
to crumble and potholes are getting
bigger.

                    EXECUTIVE DIRECTOR
Well, not in our current grant
cycle, but in the next, we will
have a pot of money that will allow
us to revamp our record-keeping
system so that the opening and
closing of client cases will be
much easier.
                    (MORE)

                    EXECUTIVE DIRECTOR (cont'd)
               (beat)
          Are there any other concerns?

The board room remains silent, eager to end the meeting.

                    EXECUTIVE DIRECTOR
          Going once, going twice, we are
          adjourned.

Employees chat in the BG as they pass behind Erica and the
E.D. and file out the boardroom.

                    ERICA
          Sorry I'm late, Boss. I would love
          to explain, but I have to be in
          court in less than 20 minutes.

                    EXECUTIVE DIRECTOR
          Not to worry. You're going places
          here, Erica.
               (matter-of-fact)
          Have you decided on the promotion
          yet?

She gives Tony a peculiar stare, then flashes a guilt-like
smile to he E.D.

                    ERICA
          Really considering. Just trying to
          hash out how I will fit my home-
          life into the new schedule.

                    EXECUTIVE DIRECTOR
          Well-

                    ERICA
          Gotta run.

She exits in a hurry. The E.D. just shrugs without concern.


**INT. PROFESSOR BARNES' OFFICE - DAY**

His lovely wife **SHARON** joins him. They've devoured lunch.

                    PROFESSOR BARNES
          She sounds like another mom that
          regrets ever leaving school to
          depend on a worthless man that
          wound up leaving on the side of the
          road.

                    SHARON
          Stand up for her. Speak to the
          board and get her back in school.
          People deserve second chances.
          Besides. You never know when you'll
          need someone to stand up for you.


**INT. PHIL KEARST'S OFFICE - DAY**

Phil is on the phone with his wife.

                    PHIL KEARST
               (to phone)
          Pretty good, Honey. Other than some
          convict trying to get a hire here.
          I don't know why the agencies
          bother sending those types over.
               (beat)
          Honey... Honey. Those kind never
          change. Once a criminal, always a
          criminal.
               (beat)
          You have a big heart, honey, but
          believe me. This guy is bad for
          society. I wouldn't trustum here.


**INT. COURT ROOM - HOLDING TANK - DAY**

The bailiff escorts Erica to her client, HEATHER RYAN, a 16
year old with tats, piercings, and streaking colors in her
hair.

Heather sits free from tension and inhibition, but Erica is
clearly disappointed with her young client.

                    ERICA
          I can't believe you!

                    HEATHER
          It was only a skirt. Why's everyone
          making such a big deal out of it?

                    ERICA
          Heather. You cannot go around
          filching skirts and think it's
          okay. Stealing is a crime and is
          recorded in your file. Any foster
          parents considering you, is privy
          to that information.

                    HEATHER
     Why don't you just adopt me?

                    ERICA
     That's not a realistic possibility.
     Fix yourself up, you're next.


**INT. COURT ROOM - DAY**

The PROSECUTOR, a shrewd, middle-aged woman stands at her box
shuffling through some folders. Her quiet, male assistant is
beside her in a chair.

Erica is awaiting Heather at the defendant's box as the
bailiff ushers her in. Heather sits, but Erica urgently
gestures her back to her feet.

The JUDGE is a sleepy-looking, prune-faced old man that is
known for occasionally dozing on the bench.

                    PROSECUTOR
     State of New Jersey, court of
     Hackensack. I, Nells Dandie,
     Prosecuting Attorney, come into set
     of Bergen County, to give the court
     to understand that, one-

Prosecutor clears her throat to awake the dozing judge. His
eyelids pop open, and he jolts gently.

                    JUDGE
     Carry on.

                    PROSECUTOR
     Heather Ryan, did walk into Mary's
     Boutique, and commit the crime of
     theft on set premises.

                    JUDGE
          (to Erica)
     Are you her lawyer. I have never
     met you, have I?

                    HEATHER
          (snazzily)
     A young girl's gotta have parents
     with plenty wealth to even consider
     such an idea as to retain paid
     legal council.

                    ERICA
               (constrained)
          I would be the Lay Advocate, your
          Honor. And no. We've never met.

                    JUDGE
          Very well. Heather Ryan?

She flashes her innocent smile -- the one she always flashes
to escape trouble.

The prosecutor is utterly annoyed by Heather's intentionally
deceitful smirk.

                    HEATHER
          That's me, your honor.

                    PROSECUTOR
          Your honor, don't be fooled by her
          cunning smile.
               (off heather's scowl)
          This is her third time before you
          in as many months.

                    ERICA
          Your Honor, my client's misconduct
          is a problem existing long before
          criminal law.

                    PROSECUTOR
          Misconduct is a soft word to
          describe harshly dishonest
          behavior.

                    ERICA
          With proper intervention and
          effective socialization we can
          recourse and mainstream my client
          into a productive citizen in our
          society.

                    PROSECUTOR
          I recommend heather Ryan be
          remanded to Wharton Track for girls
          for a minimum of one year.

Heather scowls at the prosecutor, then looks to the judge,
whom appears to be waking from another doze.

>                    ERICA
>      I recommend behavior modification
>      classes as an alternative to the
>      hardened environment of a youth
>      correctional facility.

>                  PROSECUTOR
>            (Heatedly)
>      This young lady is of
>      misdirectional intelligence and a
>      proven threat to the community.

>                    ERICA
>      Your honor. Respectfully,
>      "Misdirectional" is not a word that
>      I'm familiar with in the English
>      language, and I'm not so sure I
>      understand her point.

The prosecutor furrows as her assistant raises a pocket
dictionary to the judge, then shuffles quietly through the
pages.

>                  PROSECUTOR
>      Heather Ryan is a kleptomaniac. She
>      is a high-motor activity, and a
>      mentally troubled youth.

>                    ERICA
>      Let us not dwell at length on my
>      client's mental state, unless we
>      have made a proper diagnosis, which
>      I do not see record of in my file.
>      Not to mention, the hefty,
>      financial and legal liabilities
>      that would place upon the state, to
>      secure a treatment plan for my
>      client.

The judge pressingly awakes from yet, another doze.

>                    JUDGE
>      Nothing to sound the alarm like a
>      nice point of law.

The prosecutor's assistant nods to her, then to the judge
with disappointment and closes the pocket dictionary.

>                    JUDGE
>      Mrs. Dandie, you're an experienced
>      prosecutor.
>                (MORE)

                    JUDGE (cont'd)
          I will not tolerate the use of
          language, against a defendant, that
          cannot be defined in the English
          dictionary.

                    PROSECUTOR
               (embarrassed)
          Yes, your Honor.

The judge reviews Heather's files for a beat.

                    JUDGE
          Mrs. Lake, the court of Hackensack,
          in the state of New Jersey, has not
          made a proper diagnosis of your
          client, Heather Ryan. Therefore, a
          treatment plan is not in place, and
          the state cannot intelligently
          measure or sentence a punishment
          upon your client, based on remarks
          of her mental state, by the
          prosecution. With that said, the
          court shall release Heather Ryan to
          the responsibility of her Lay
          Advocate, and the representing
          agency. Subsequently, the court
          hopes that the Lay Advocate will
          have her client properly diagnosed
          in the very near future.

                    ERICA
               (victory grin)
          Absolutely, your Honor.

                    JUDGE
               (BANGS his gavel)
          Case dismissed!

                    HEATHER
               (to Erica; sly)
          You should be lawyer.

The prosecutor plops into her chair disappointedly.


**EXT. SOMEWHERE IN NJ - MEDICINAL DISTRICT - DAY**

Chad enters a swank private structure through automatic
doors.

He stands in the entrance-hall for a beat, scanning the
people in the building with no real particular interest.

Chad seems a little uncertain, like a cloud is over is head.

> CHAD (V.O.)
> I strive to be a better person, but
> it's a struggle. My feet just
> aren't beneath me. Sometimes the
> pressures of choice is so intense.
> Sometimes. I want to end it all.
> Just to avoid having to choose.
> Ever felt like that?

Chad walks slowly, almost reluctantly, to the elevator.


## INT. RECEPTION ROOM - DAY

Chad approaches sliding double-windows, where RECEPTIONIST #2
is seen closing-out a phone call. She hangs up and slides the
window back.

> RECEPTIONIST #2
> (to Chad; friendly)
> Good afternoon, how can I help you?

> CHAD
> Chad Miller. 2pm appointment with
> Dr. Sean Levin.

> RECEPTIONIST #2
> Okay. Identification and insurance
> card, please.

Chad gathers the requested information and hands it to her.

> RECEPTIONIST #2
> Thank you. Just have a seat. I will
> zerox this, and let Dr. Levin know
> you're here.

> CHAD
> (as he sits)
> Thank you.

She closes the sliding window and dials Dr. Levin's
extension.

> RECEPTIONIST #2
> (to phone)
> Chad Miller is here to see you.

**INT. DR. SEAN LEVIN'S OFFICE - DAY**

He's completing case notes in his computer files, with his
phone on speaker.

>                    DR. LEVIN
>          That client should have been
>          referred out. I'm not taking
>          anymore medicaid clients.

>                    RECEPTIONIST #2
>               (through phone)
>          I guess there was some confusion
>          with the new intake worker. I will
>          inform the client. Sorry.

>                    DR. LEVIN
>          Thank you.
>               (clicks speaker off;
>                examine notes; sotto)
>          Hmm. What date was that?

Dr. Levin slides back in his chair... swings his office door
open... steps into the corridor.

As Dr. passes the receptionist desk an employee attempts to
stop him and show some documents that he emphatically, has no
time to look at. The employee is disappointed with the Dr.'s
haste.

>                    DR. LEVIN
>          I have to run to the file room.
>          Stick it in my mailbox.

>                    RECEPTIONIST #2
>               (to chad)
>          I'm so sorry about the mix-up. Use
>          this list of referrals, and I'm
>          sure you'll find someone who will
>          see you.

Dr. Levin stops at the receptionist desk. He stares as Chad
accepts the referrals.

Dr. Levin eyes squint curiously at a dejected Chad, the man
whom he almost had a violent encounter with, just yesterday.

As Chad is about to turn and walk away-

>                    DR. LEVIN
>          Wait! Are you Chad Miller...?

                    CHAD
Yes...
     (surprised)
Are you Dr. Levin?

                    DR. LEVIN
I am.
     (to receptionist #2)
Process the paper work. I'll see
him.

Chad and Dr. Levin exchange chummy stares.


## EXT. URBAN AMERICA - UPTOWN - DAY

Seedy storefronts and broken-up sidewalks. The crowd is less
frenzied and not as classy as the downtown crowd.

Chad stops in the middle of the street as a mangy car putt-
putts by, its loose muffler CLANGING against the pavement,
DRAGGING a trail of sparks.

The loud HISS of air-brakes from a public bus startle a
jittery, stray mutt as Chad waves the fog of emissions from
his face.

Chad crosses the street where he flirts with a couple of
shapely women and takes a phone number from one, then he
enters a local pub called One West.

                    CHAD (V.O.)
          I told the Dr. About Erica and
          Lana, my wife. My love for them
          both, and my inability to choose
          one over the other, for different
          reasons. And the difficulty I am
          having living with it. Erica is
          right. My behavior is changing, and
          a new me is emerging. Just a new me
          with many of same ways. And that's
          not the me I wanna be.


## INT. ONE WEST - DAY

An under-decorated pub, dimly lit. Outdated stools and
tables. No patrons in the front area.

Until we hear VOICES from the back, we're not sure anyone is
in the joint.

Ice cubes CLINK into a Glass. A bottle-top UNSCREWS. Scotch POURS over the ice cubes causing them to CLINK again.

A match STRIKES and flares. The small glow of fire moves toward a cigarette and lights it, revealing the silhouette of **CHARLIE,** the bartender. A lean balding man.

Charlie drags his cigarette, then blows smoke. His crossed eyes appear unfocused, but you can trust he's tuned-in to his surroundings.

At the back pool table, Chad and a few childhood buddies hold a friendly game over some brews. Chad sets up for his shot.

                    BUDDY #1
          Chad, you're different.

                    BUDDY #2
               (rhetorical)
          You know what I'm saying. I don't
          know who this cat is nowadays.

                    BUDDY #3
          Still a lover, maybe. But the new
          Chad is calm. Humble. Maybe a bit
          soft.

                    CHAD
               (grins)
          Whoa. That's defamation of
          character.

Chad's buddies let out taunting laughter.

                    BUDDY #1
          Yeah. He's soft. Cause he might of
          shot you dead in "86" for
          defamation of character.

Chad reaches behind his back pretending to draw a gun. His buddies reach for the sky, pretending to submit.

The guys fall into laughter. Charlie's even grinning across the bar. He likes to see the guys have a good time.

Erica enters the bar. She waves to Charlie and gestures him to stay quiet so she can surprise Chad.

                    BUDDY #1
          Yall ever see that R. Kelly sex
          video?

                    CHAD
          Not interested in child
          pornography.

                    ERICA
          Good answer.

Surprised by the female voice out of nowhere, the guys all
stare at Erica, then exchange embarrassed glares.

                    ERICA
          You sound like a bunch of
          predators. R. Kelly needs
          psychiatric help. And if any of you
          are anything like him, then you
          need psychiatric help too.

                    BUDDY #3
          Predators?

                    BUDDY #1
                (offended)
          Psychiatric Help?

                    ERICA
          Grown men liking young girls is
          diagnosable. It's called
          pedophilia.
                (eyes still on the guys)
          Chad are you ready?

                    CHAD
          I just got one more shot.
                (off Erica's look)
          But I'm ready.


**EXT. DOWNTOWN - BUSINESS DISTRICT - DAY**

Stylish business-like pedestrians are pushing and rushing
through while others converse at sidewalk shops.

Finally, We come to an office building, STAR ENTERTAINMENT.
Erica Double parks, and Chad jumps out her car, then turns to
the passenger window.

                    CHAD
          Come in with me.

                    ERICA
          There's nowhere for me to park. And
          I'm tired. I wanna go home.

                    CHAD
          Alright. You had a long day.

                    ERICA
               (firm)
          Stay out the hoodlum bar!
               (needy)
          And come see about me later

                    CHAD
               (blows a kiss)
          I will.


## INT. STAR ENTERTAINMENT - SHELLY'S OFFICE - DAY

Chad enters. Shelly closes the door. She appears hurried and
busy.


                    SHELLY
          Have a seat.
               (to phone)
          Is Carl Thomas available to sing
          the national anthem on Friday or
          Sunday for the Nets playoff game?
               (beat)
          Ten grand, flight, hotel, court
          side tickets.
               (beat)
          For ten grand he can learn the
          words.

Her cell phone RINGS. She's annoyed. She gestures for Chad to
grab it from her purse.


                    SHELLY
               (to land line)
          Hold on.
               (to cellular)
          Look, you're gunnuh lose your
          deposit. You have three days to
          come up with $11,000, or the 15
          grand you already put down is gone -
          - 12 to Mario and three to me.
               (beat)
          Well, you'd better work quick.

She ends the call.

                    SHELLY
               (to land line)
          Hello. Hello!
                    (MORE)

                   SHELLY (cont'd)
           (beat)
       Guess he hung up.

She hangs up and takes a deep breath.

                   SHELLY
           (to Chad)
       This shit has been going on all
       day.

                   CHAD
       Sorry to pop up unannounced. You
       got a minute?

                   SHELLY
       yeah, what's up?

                   CHAD
       I have a revision for you.

                   SHELLY
       My source is already interested. He
       loves the story. You can expect a
       pretty nice check soon.

                   CHAD
       Yeah?

                   SHELLY
       Yeah. This thing is really looking
       up.

                   CHAD
       Beautiful! Your the best.

The phones ring again. Shelly is livid.

                   SHELLY
       I need to go to lunch.


**EXT. PARK VIEW TERRACE - BLUE COLLAR COMMUNITY - DAY**

Two level fixed-income apartments. We hear SNORES WHISTLE
from the BANKS apartment.

**INT. BANKS LIVING ROOM - DAY**

**WOODROW BANKS**, forty-something, is sprawled in his recliner.
His gaping mouth unleash HEAVY SNORES. Tiny crow-feet lines
spread the corners of his bagged-filled eyes.

He's still wearing his shop uniform. The shirt fully
unbuttoned. Sweat-circles stain the pit of his underarms. An
oscillating fan WHIFFS across him.

On the end table <u>You and I</u>, by Rick James, CROONS from a 70's
portable radio with a makeshift antenna.

Beside the radio is a vintage picture and frame of Woodrow in
the army. He was only 17 then.

The apartment is of wretched walls, worn-out chairs, and ugly
curtains. An exposed lamp of low wattage lends heavily to the
apartment's smutty look.

A light haze of smoke rises from a burning cigarette in the
ashtray. An empty drinking glass sits beside a half-filled
vodka bottle.

We hear Laboring FOOTSTEPS coming from the upper staircase.
**ROSINA BANKS** reaches the bottom and steps into OUR FRAME.
She's a short round woman in her early 40's.

Rosina has a challenging look about her. Her face is deep
south all the way. She's wearing a fogy cotton nightgown with
a cheap head-scarf.

She presses her palm to the wall for support and catches her
breath.

Woodrow's snoring stops momentarily. Then a sudden SCOURING
noise grabs our attention.

Rosina looks right and sees Woodrow with one hand down his
pants, SCRATCHING his crotch with rapid motion.

Still in a slumber, Woodrow sniffs the flaky incrustation in
his fingers nails. His face crinkles at the frowzy smell,
then his SNORING resumes.

Rosina is skeeved, and her face crinkles too. She shakes her
head as if she's lost all hope and confidence in her irksome
husband.

Rosina crosses to the kitchen. The music fades.


**INT. BANKS KITCHEN - DAY**

Spatters of old grease dash the wall just above the burners.
Used cooking grease is stored in jars lined across the
counter. Makeshift labels read, "FISH" and "CHICKEN." Mucky
dishes pile the small sink.

Rosina swings opens the outdated fridge. It's empty of basic contents. A nearly depleted kool-aid container. Two beer bottles. Two small pots. One covered, and the other exposed, revealing day old corn.

Rosina's eyes roll with disappointment. She looks downward to the lower shelf. Her pudgy hand grabs a package of deli cuts.

She shuts the fridge and grabs a generic bread bag off the counter. Only the end slices remain. She scowls with more disappointment.

                    ROSINA
               (sotto)
          I don't believe this.

She wobbles out the kitchen and crosses to the living room where Woodrow is still SNORING.

## INT. LIVING ROOM - DAY

Woodrow's face slumps lazily. Drool sneaks from the corner of his mouth. Rosina's brow furrows with disgust.

She stubs out his cigarette in the ashtray. She CLICKS off the radio, and then she yanks him by the shirt collar.

                    ROSINA
          Woodrow! Get up, Woodrow! You hear
          me!

Woodrow efforts to escape his drunken stupor. He realizes it's his annoying wife holding him, and the tension in his face increases as his road-map eyes stretch wide open.

Woodrow yanks himself free of her grip. His eyes blinking rabidly with annoyance.

His southern broken-English coupled with his drunken Yiddish is comical to hear, but almost makes you feel sorry for the guy.

                    WOODROW
          Whut, woman? Git'cho hands off me.

                    ROSINA
          Don't bat those bloodshot eyes at
          me. And don't *whut* me either!
          Where's the bread, Woodrow?

                    WOODROW
          Whut bread?

                    ROSINA
          The bread I sent you to the store
          to buy eight o' clock this morning?

He flags her off.

                    ROSINA
          Now it's one o'clock in the
          afternoon, Woodrow.

                    WOODROW
          I ain't been to no store, and I
          ain't seent no bread.

                    ROSINA
               (grabs the vodka bottle)
          You got this devilish alcohol! You
          been to the store. You gone drink
          yourself to death. The doctor told
          you to quit drinking, Woodrow.

She SLAMS the bottle back on the table. Woodrow twitches with
drunken animation. His movements, just as his speech, comical
but sad. The trail of drool drips down his sagging jowls.

                    WOODROW
          I ain't saying I ain't been to da'
          store. I'm saying I ain't been to
          da' store and seent no bread.

                    ROSINA
          You see what time it is?
               (points to wall clock)
          Look at the clock, Woodrow! What
          does the clock say?

                    WOODROW
          N- now, look here. The clock say he
          ain't been to da' store,' and he
          ain't seent no bread either.

Woodrow SNICKERS, really tickling himself.

                    ROSINA
               (jabs her finger)
          You best get your act together,
          Mister. You need to be at work,
          instead of sitting around here
          scouring your filthy balls.

                    WOODROW
          Whut act you talkin' bout woman? I
          took one half-day off. Sides that.
               (MORE)

                    WOODROW (cont'd)
I werks. I gits up five days'ah
week, and I werks. Make sure dis'
rent iz paid. And I make sure yah
big ass eats. And you know you's ah
eatin' ass.

                    ROSINA
First off, Woodrow. Don't call me
"big-ass." Secondly. I work too.
And I contribute just as much to
the bills as you do.

                    WOODROW
Oh...? Why da' fone bill ain't paid
den -- huh?

                    ROSINA
Hush about the phone. You just wipe
that shit from around your mouth.
And hand me the money I gave you
for the bread?

He runs his sleeve across his mouth, clearing the drool.

                    WOODROW
I ain't got no money for no bread.

                    ROSINA
You bought liquor with it, didn't
you?

                    WOODROW
Azackly!

                    ROSINA
I can't even make myself a descent
sandwich. I'm so hungry I got gas.
        (holding stomach;
         flagellates loudly)
Ooh! Excuse me.

                    WOODROW
        (grimace with disgust)
Aw, Rosina! Whut you go an do dat
fo! Dats such'ah gotdam turnoff!

                    ROSINA
Shut up. That's natural. You drink
too much!

              WOODROW
       Yeah? And you eat too damn much!
       Now vanish. Disappear.

That moment, door locks TURN and CLICK, then the front door
opens and closes OFF SCREEN. Footsteps follow. Rosina waves
Woodrow off hurriedly

              ROSINA
       Shh! That's Lisa.

**LISA BANKS** enters the living room. She's an attractive
sixteen year old dressed in urban fashion.

Tight jeans reveal her curves. Construction boots display her
edge. And a pink jacket lends to her femininity.

              LISA
       Hi, mommy.

              ROSINA
       Hey, baby. You're home early.

              LISA
       Half-day. You look angry. Fighting
       again?

              ROSINA
       No. Just get your clothes ready for
       school tomorrow.

              LISA
        (whatever)
       Tomorrow is Saturday. And I work
       tonight. Are you okay, mommy?

              ROSINA
        (hiding her anger)
       Everything is fine.

              LISA
        (not convinced)
       I'm leaving.

Lisa turns and exits the living room in a huff. The front
door CREAKS open then SLAMS shut.

Rosina stares at the space where Lisa just stood. Her face
saddened, and her eyes shine with a glossy emergence.

**EXT. PARK VIEW TERRACE - COMPLEX PLAYGROUND - DAY**

Lisa plops on a bench beside her best friend, STEPHANIE
CADENO. Stephanie can tell Lisa is unhappy.

> STEPHANIE
> How'd it go?

> LISA
> It didn't go.

> STEPHANIE
> You didn't tell them?

> LISA
> They don't have any time for my
> problems. They have their own.

> STEPHANIE
> What are you going to do?

> LISA
> I don't know.

> STEPHANIE
> I heard Kenneth already has a baby
> with Yvonne, and he doesn't support
> them very much. Did you know that?

> LISA
> I knew Yvonne had a baby girl. But
> I didn't know it was by Kenneth.
> Guess he told her to keep it a
> secret, too.

> STEPHANIE
> Yep. Because he's 23 and she's 16.
> Same as you.

> LISA
> A grown man running game on teenage
> girls. Shame, shame, shame.

> STEPHANIE
> You ask him if was going to help
> you support the baby?

> LISA
> I did.

> STEPHANIE
> What'd he say?

Lisa throws her arms and shoulders to mimic Kenneth's macho
behavior.

>                    LISA
>          "Word is bond, Lisa. Ahma take
>          care' ah mine."

>                    STEPHANIE
>              (tickled)
>          You're so silly.

>                    LISA
>              (grinning)
>          That's how he said it.

>                    STEPHANIE
>          You believe him?

>                    LISA
>          Hell no. The proof is in the
>          pudding.

>                    STEPHANIE
>          I wonder if Yvonne knows about you?

>                    LISA
>          I don't know.


**EXT. URBAN STREET - DAY**

Ragged cars parked on the street. Tattered garbage cans and
piles of trash-bags are tossed carelessly about the curbside.
The houses are dumpy with unkept lawns.

A yard mechanic works on a HOOPTY in the driveway. Tools
CLINK and a ratchet WINDS.

A mangy old dog scurries to a worn fence, and into our view.
It struggles to let out a series of raspy BARKS.

Across the street, **YVONNE** and a group of teenage girls cipher
on the porch of a shabby two family house.

Yvonne is an attractive teen with a spicy attitude, and she
is extremely unhappy. Almost in tears. Yvonne contemplates
ringing the bell but isn't sure.

Her girlfriends incite her and rally her on. Yvonne presses
the bell. She presses it again. Then she presses once more
out of pure adrenaline.

We hear a window RUMBLE open from the top half of the house.

**KENNETH**, with a head full of corn rows, pokes his head out
the window. He overlooks the empty street.

                    KENNETH
          Yo...! Who dat!?

He waits for his visitor to come off the porch and onto the
front walkway where he can see them.

Yvonne steps from the porch and into view. She stares up at
him with displeased mannerisms.

Kenneth is agitated. Not so much with the unexpected company.
But more so because he can tell from her posture that he's in
for another verbal battle.

Kenneth throws up one finger and holds it briefly, indicating
he needs a minute. He draws back from the window and
disappears into the house.

Moments later Kenneth steps out onto the porch. He's in beach
slippers with no shirt, displaying his weak frame. He's
surprised to see the group of girls accompanying Yvonne.

Kenneth seems apprehensive. He looks this way, then that way.

                    YVONNE
               (sarcastic)
          The coast is clear. No cops.

                    KENNETH
             (whatever)
          What's up, Yvonne?

                    YVONNE
          Besides the child support you're
          not paying?!

Stressed with the verbal attack, Kenneth fails to answer.

                    YVONNE
          You fucked Lisa...!? And you didn't
          use protection? Now that bitch is
          pregnant?

                    KENNETH
          We're not together. You broke up
          with me.

                    YVONNE
Yeah, because you wouldn't get a
job and handle your
responsibilities. Not because I
wanted to sleep around.


                    KENNETH
You was actin' funny on me. Holding
out.


                    YVONNE
          (desolate)
I loved you, Kenneth. I still love
you. How could you? Another
baby...? Kenneth!?


                    KENNTH
          (reactionary)
You wouldn't gimmie none. She did.
Can I live? Damn!


                    HOME GIRL #1
          (shakes her head)
I see why you only prey on teenage
girls. Cause no grown ass woman
would tolerate your ignorance.


                    KENNETH
Step. It's my life. What's the big
deal?


                    YVONNE
The big deal, asshole... is you got
another child on the way, but
you're not taking care of the one
you already have.


                    KENNETH
          (angry)
Man, you got my licensed suspended
and shit with this child support.
Got warrants out for my arrest.
Try'na get money outta' me I ain't
got.


                    YVONNE
It's not my child, Kenneth. It's
our child. If I gotta find a way to
make it happen, then so do you!


Yvonne wells up with fury. Here eyes search for understanding
from Kenneth. He only stares blankly.

She grows emotionally charged and disgusted with his infidelity and resigned attitude.

She SPITS in his face -- more out of rage than courage. He's shocked initially. Then anger sets in.

                    KENNETH
          You spit in my face, yo!?

                    YVONNE
               (despair)
          I know it's low-down and
          disrespectful. But so is cheating
          on me and your daughter, you
          bastard!

                    KENNTH
               (wiping face)
          I don't wanna hear that shit!

                    HOME GIRL #1
               (intervenes)
          Calm down, big bro. Don't make my
          girl feel threatened.

                    KENNETH
          Move out the way, bitch!

Kenneth shoves girlfriend #1 aside and mushes Yvonne's face with his palm, nearly knocking her to the ground. Yvonne's girlfriends are enraged!

They attack Kenneth rabidly with hard punches, kicks and slaps, scratches and bites.

Kenneth THUDS to the porch floor, and he's shocked to be on his ass, beaten by girls.

                    GIRLFRIEND #1
          Don't you put your punk ass hands
          on her!

The mangy dog BARKS madly from across the street. The yard mechanic slides from under the car to see what's all the commotion, and he cringes in humor at Kenneth's ass-kicking by a group of teenage girls.

Kenneth attempts to climb to his feet, but a solid blow to the jaw sends him back on his ass. His nose and mouth bloodied. His body nicked, scarred, and bruised pretty good.

Kenneth is disoriented. Girlfriend #1 stands over him.

GIRLFRIEND #1
We don't run from domestic
violence. We handle it.

The other girlfriend's comment in the BG and slap high-fives.
Yvonne is off to the side. She stares with impressed
disbelief.


## INT. LISA'S LIVINGROOM - DAY

Lisa nurse Kenneth's wounds with a wet rag. Stephanie stares
nervously.

LISA
Omigosh, baby! Are you okay?

KENNTH
(pushing rag away)
Yeah, I'm good. I just came to warn
you. This chic is loopy.

Lisa sits affectionately on his lap. Woodrow peeks in the
living room. He looks displeased with the seating
arrangement. He scowls and turns away.

STEPHANIE
You shouldn't have gotten Lisa
mixed up in this, Kenneth.

LISA
She's right. You should have told
me about Yvonne. And gave me the
chance to decide for or against.

Woodrow pokes his head back into the living room, and Lisa is
still on Kenneth's lap.

WOODROW
Look here! I know it got to be
more'den one seat in here.

LISA
(embarrassed)
Daddy...?

WOODROW
It's gettin' late and school
tomorra'-

LISA
It's not late, and there's no
school tomorrow, Daddy!

>           WOODROW
> I don't give'ah shit. Skool r' no
> skool. Company, and everybody,
> split!

## EXT. PARK VIEW TERRACE - COMPLEX PLAYGROUND - DAY

Lisa hugs Kenneth and kisses his cheek.

>           LISA
> Sorry about my dad.

>           KENNTH
> It's cool.

>           LISA
> Be safe. See you tomorrow?

>           KENNTH
> Yeah. You be safe too. Stay close
> to home until this chic and her
> crew calms down.

>           LISA
> Okay.

Kenneth walks off. Stephanie and Lisa sit on the bench.

>           STEPHANIE
> You really like him, don't you?

>           LISA
> I do. I think he loves me, but I
> also think he's no damn good.

>           LISA
> You sound confused to me.

>           LISA
> I am confused.

We hear CACKLING and BICKERING coming from over the shrubbery
at the other end of the playground.

>           LISA
> Ms. Lucy and fat Drake are fussing
> again.

>           STEPHANIE
> What do they fuss so much about?

                    LISA
Any and everything. But mostly over
checkers.

                    STEPHANIE
They're crazy.

                    LISA
Tell me about it.

                    STEPHANIE
You think Yvonne is gunnuh' fight
you over this?

                    LISA
I hope not. I didn't know he was
with her.

                    STEPHANIE
            (checks watch)
Almost time for work.

                    LISA
What time do you have be back at
the group home.

                    STEPHANIE
They know I'm off at 11, so I have
an hour travel time.

                    LISA
Sure hope I don't see Yvonne.

They rise from the bench and start toward the other end of
the playground.


**EXT. COMPLEX PLAYGROUND - OVER THE SHRUBBERY - DAY**

**MS. LUCY** and **DRAKE** Play a game of checkers at the picnic
table. They're a comical duo.

Ms. Lucy sits tactless with a head full of hair-curlers. Her
battered legs of decade-old scars emerge from a worn-down
nightie.

She's loud, nosey, informed, and a tart-tongued sass mouth.
Ms. Lucy is only 41, but the lines in her face tell an older
story.

Drake sits across from her. His popped-belly pressed against
the picnic table.

At age fifty his hair already fully gray, and his eyes squint
through thick glasses.

Drake stares at the checker board with intense study. His
cordless phone lay on the table beside his cola.

>           MS. LUCY
> It ain't Quantum Physics. It's just
> checkers.  No matter where you
> move, it's over.

Her pressure works. He lifts his arm. He holds it steady,
still thinking over his move.

>           DRAKE
>      (annoyed)
> Quit rushing me, Lucy.  I don't say
> nothin' to you when you thinking.

>           MS. LUCY
> I'm bout' to wax that ass, Drake.
> You can get comfortable with the
> notion, or you can cry like a baby.

He slides his checker to the next square. He snaps his arm
back with confidence. He believes he made the right move.

>           DRAKE
> Mm-hm. Now what?

She double jumps him.

>           MS. LUCY
> Study long, study wrong. Hah!

>           DRAKE
>      (irked)
> That's the only way you can win.
> Keep on rushing me.

>           MS. LUCY
> I ain't rushing you.

>           DRAKE
> You are rushing me, Lucy. You
> applying pressure.

>           MS. LUCY
> You make it so easy. Crybaby.

>           DRAKE
> Start over.

The girls are striding pass Ms. Lucy and Drake when Drake
suddenly jumps up from the table with his high derriere
climbing his back, and he playfully reaches for Stephanie.

Stephanie leans into Lisa. Her arms drawn to her chest.

                    DRAKE
          C'mear girl.

                    STEPHANIE
          Get outta here, Drake.

                    DRAKE
          Girl, you can have my whole
          dislability check.

                    MS. LUCY
          It's dis-a-bility, fool.

                    DRAKE
               (lustful)
          She know what I mean.

                    LISA
               (teasing)
          Stephanie. You know you like him.

                    STEPHANIE
          I don't think so.

                    MS. LUCY
          Lisa, You ain't been looking too
          well lately. I seen you spittin' up
          a couple mornings, on your way to
          school. Everything okay?

                    LISA
               (embarrassed)
          Uh! Yeah, Ms. Lucy. I wasn't
          feeling well.

                    MS. LUCY
          I noticed. What's wrong, sugar?

                    LISA
          I need glasses.

                    MS. LUCY
          Glasses?

                    LISA
          Yep. I need glasses.

> MS. LUCY
> You young folk think you can just
> tell us old folk anything, huh?

> LISA
> No, really. I do need glasses.
> Right, Stephanie?
>     (nudges Stephanie)
> Right, Stephanie?!

> STEPHANIE
> Oh! Yeah! That's what she told me.

Lisa strains a nervous smile. Ms. Lucy's eyes drift down to Lisa's stomach.

> MS. LUCY
> Well. You better hurry up and get
> those glasses. Or tell that boy to
> marry you.

Lisa's eyes bug. Her body immobilized. She's iffy about staying quiet, or providing another useless defense.

> MS. LUCY
> That's all. You can go.

Lisa hooks Stephanie by the arm and heads back toward the playground.

**EXT. PARK VIEW TERRACE - PLAYGROUND**

Lisa drops to the bench with shame. She tugs Stephanie by the elbow.

> LISA
> We're not leaving yet. Sit back
> down.

> STEPHANIE
> I don't want to sit down. I want to
> go to work.

> LISA
> We don't have to be in for another
> hour and change.
>     (tugs Stephanie harder)
> Just sit!

Stephanie's neck jerks as she falls onto the bench. She rubs the back of her neck with a grimace.

                    STEPHANIE
          Whoa!


                    LISA
          I am so found out. How does she
          know?

                    STEPHANIE
          Maybe, because teenage girls don't
          usually spit-up when they need
          glasses.  Duh!

                    LISA
          She might tell my parents.

                    STEPHANIE
          She might.

                    LISA
          This is not good.

Just then, Lisa hears her parents arguing in the BG. She
looks toward her apartment, then turns away.

                    LISA
          Will you come with me to the
          clinic?

                    STEPHANIE
          You wanna start your prenatal?

                    LISA
          No! I'm going to the A.B. Clinic.

Lisa lifts her shirt to examine her stomach. Stephanie rubs
her belly.

                    STEPHANIE
          What are you, two months?

                    LISA
          Yeah.

                    STEPHANIE
          That's how far I was. If you're
          going to kill it. It's best to do
          it early, I guess.

                    LISA
               (distressed)
          I don't want to kill it.

                    STEPHANIE
               (apologetic)
          I didn't mean to say kill it. Did I
          say kill it?

                    LISA
               (she sobs)
          Whatever you're trying to say it
          isn't helping.

                    STEPHANIE
          I'm so sorry. I was just trying to
          share my experience with you so you
          wouldn't feel so isolated with
          yours.

Lisa leans into Stephanie with a stressful sigh.

                    STEPHANIE
          You should talk to Erica.

                    LISA
          My neighbor?

                    STEPHANIE
          Yeah. She's a counselor, or
          something.


## INT. ERICA'S APARTMENT - DAY

Erica and the girls sit at the dinning table.

                    ERICA
          You really need to tell your
          parents.

                    LISA
          I can never catch them when they're
          not screaming about their own
          problems. How did this happen to
          me? It was my first time.

                    ERICA
          Here's what I think. A female's
          peak for pregnancy is between the
          ages of 15-22. So. That whole
          hormonal, high-sex-drive thing.
          It's sort of ingrained. The trick.
          Is to know how to moderate it.

                    STEPHANIE
          Like how? Know when, and when not
          to be horny?

                      ERICA
          No, silly. That button you can't
          control. But what you can control
          is giving yourself alternative
          things to do besides being alone
          with boys.

                      LISA
          I know. We're too young to be
          thinking about boys, right?

                      ERICA
          I'm not saying separate yourself
          from your male friends. But
          understand, just because you date,
          doesn't mean you need to have sex
          every chance you're alone.
          Relationships are so much more than
          that.


**EXT. MEDICAL CENTER - DAY**

EMT's rush a wounded teen through the automatic doors and
into the trauma center.


**INT. MEDICAL CENTER - DAY**

We TRACK through the corridor... pass the busy nurses
station... and into a quiet, still room.

Professor Barnes stands over his gravely ill wife. He
clutches her hand and stares mournfully at all the tubes,
monitors, and supports that she's hooked up to.

The **PRIMARY PHYSICIAN** steps in, patient file in hand, and a
clipboard.

                    PRIMARY PHYSICIAN
               (low voice)
          Mr. Barnes.

                    PROFESSOR BARNES
               (he turns)
          Yes?

The Doctor gestures him to step outside the room. We follow
the two men slowly down the corridor.

                    PRIMARY PHYSICIAN
The procedure would be considered a
precautionary measure, and not one
we can justify as ultimately
necessary for treatment.

                    PROFESSOR BARNES
          (angry)
Which means my insurance won't
cover.

                    PRIMARY PHYSICIAN
They can. But you have to convince
them that the procedure can
potentially be the difference
between life or death.
          (off Professor Barnes
          look)
Here's the a copy of her file. You
have a good case.

Professor barnes stops the doctor as he turns to walk away.

                    PROFESSOR BARNES
But couldn't you better explain
this so sudden illness to my
insurance company.

                    PRIMARY PHYSICIAN
Now, the matter is between you and
them. It's really out of my hands.

                    PROFESSOR BARNES
But, Dr...?

                    PRIMARY PHYSICIAN
I understand your pain, sir. But
it's not a decision I have the
power to make.

                    PROFESSOR BARNES
          (desperate)
But you do have the power, Dr. If
you truly understand my pain, then
convince the insurance company that
your patient... this mother... my
wife... needs a chance. Please.
This could determine the difference
between an untimely death, or ten
more years of life.

The Dr. Takes the file from Professor Barnes' hand.

>                    PRIMARY PHYSICIAN
>                     (compassionate)
>             I'll do what I can do to stand up
>             for you.

Professor Barnes' eyes read with gratitude, But his face droops with guilt. And we know why.


## INT. CHAD'S HOUSE - MASTER BEDROOM - DAY

We hear the CREAK of a rocking chair against the wide plank floor. It's Lana, rocking Chad Jr to sleep.


## INT. KITCHEN - CHAD'S HOUSE - DAY

JOY is at the single-serve fusion station, brewing coffee for mommy.

Sabrina and Diana are pleasing themselves at the breakfast nook with large bowls of fudge swirl ice cream.

Chad enters the kitchen and the girls rush him with hugs and hugs and excitement. Chad adores the love, and gives each of the girls a kiss.

>                        CHAD
>             On my way out, but I'll be back.

>                        JOY
>                     (disappointed)
>             Where you going, Daddy?

>                        CHAD
>             Just gotta make a quick run.

>                        DIANA
>             What time you coming home?

>                        CHAD
>             I don't know.


## INT. MASTER BEDROOM - CHAD'S HOUSE - DAY

Lana is dozing off, reluctantly beating Chad Jr to sleep. Chad taps the wall gently. She lifts her heavy eyelids.

Chad steps softly over, careful not to arouse the toddler who's still not quiet asleep.

                    CHAD
               (soft)
          I'll be back.

                    LANA
          What time?

                    CHAD
               (casual irritation; still
                soft)
          I don't know.

                    LANA
          Well, where you going?

                    CHAD
               (More irritated)
          I don't know. Just out.

                    LANA
          Whatever.

Chad kisses the baby on the cheek.

                    CHAD
          See you later, son.

                    CHAD JR
          Bye, Da-dee.

                    LANA
          I don't get a good-bye kiss?

He kisses her cheek in a huff.

                    LANA
               (hurt)
          You don't have to be so irked.

                    CHAD (V.O.)
          I truly love Lana, and desire to
          spend more time with my family.
          Lana has done so right by me, but
          Erica is in my system.

Lana gives him a quiet steady look. Behind her beauty, around
her glossy eyes, we can see the fateful pain caused by her
private fear of Chad having an affair.

Chad's eyes are apologetic and damn near guilty. His head
shakes disappointingly to suggest Lana's got the wrong idea.

                         LANA
                    (disdain)
               Tell her I said hi.

                         CHAD
               Baby, it's not what you're
               thinking.

                         LANA
                    (not convinced)
               Just go.


## INT. ERICA'S APARTMENT - DINING ROOM - DAY

Erica and the girls finish their talk over soup and
sandwiches.

There's an 8.5 X 11 photo of Erica and her four year old
girl, BRIA. Stephanie admires the photo.

                         STEPHANIE
               Awwww... how cute.

                         ERICA
                    (she smiles)
               That's my baby.

                         STEPHANIE
               Where is she?

                         ERICA
               With her dad.

                         LISA
               I can't believe I let myself get
               into this stupid situation.

                         ERICA
               You're young, and you're a girl.
               Young girls do silly things. I've
               been there.

                         LISA
               I just don't feel good about this.

                         ERICA
               I'm not saying it's okay, but
               things happen.

                         STEPHANIE
               She said she thinks he's no good,
               but she think he loves her.

                    LISA
               (annoyed)
          I also said I was confused.

                    STEPHANIE
          Okay. I'm sorry.

                    ERICA
               (to Lisa)
          That's normal. Maybe he's showing
          you two emotions, which is causing
          that confusing.

                    LISA
          Sometimes he's the dog I believe he
          is, but other times he's the
          surprising, Prince Charming.


                    ERICA
          And you'd rather believe he can
          eventually become Prince Charming,
          instead of remain the "Dog?"

                    LISA
          I guess. My life is so out of
          control now.

                    ERICA
          It's not what yo go through that
          makes or breaks you. It's how you
          handle it. So toughen up. It's
          decision time.

                    STEPHANIE
          I've been pregnant before. By an
          older guy as well. Much older than
          Lisa's Kenneth. That's why my dad
          stuck me in the girls home.

Quiet beat. Erica rubs Stephanie across the shoulders.

                    ERICA
          When you're young, you're daring. A
          little bold, a little stupid --
          willing to try anything once or
          twice.

Erica gets up and begins clearing the table.

                    LISA
          What were you like when you were
          our age?

                    STEPHANIE
          I bet she was conceited.

                    ERICA
          I wasn't conceited, blatantly, but
          in my heart I thought I was, "All
          that," which really wasn't helpful
          to me.

Erica ponders a short beat as she wipes down the table.

                    ERICA
          Everything I knew about the world
          as a teen, I thought was all there
          was, and I took a few bumps and
          bruises for it.

                    LISA
               (sad)
          We're not going to work out. I
          should get rid of his baby.

                    ERICA
          This is such a difficult choice at
          such a young age. But I say you
          don't get rid of it because it's
          his. You keep it because it yours.

                    LISA
          I never thought of it quite like
          that.

                    STEPHANIE
          Well, if she has the baby, but
          still earns her degree, then life
          will still be a success, right.

                    ERICA
               (guilty)
          Honestly -- nothing's a guarantee.
          But, going to college and <u>finishing</u>
          surely lessons the odds of an
          uncertain future.

                    LISA
               (proud)
          I was accepted to N.Y.U.

                    ERICA
               (excited)
          Really!? You must have aced your
          SAT's?

                    LISA
          1400. Baby or not, my master's is
          the minimum. Criminal law major.


                    ERICA
          Wow! You should feel good about
          yourself.

Erica's home phone RINGS. The girls get up.

                    STEPHANIE
          Take your call. We have to go to
          work.

Erica waves bye as she answers her phone. The girls let
themselves out.

                    ERICA
               (to phone)
          Hello.
               (beat; annoyed)
          Just a regular ass work day.
          Nothing exciting.
               (beat)
          I need a check. Are you going to
          write it?
               (long beat)
          She's in day care, she's in dance
          class, she goes to Kumon. None of
          that's free.
               (beat)
          Every time I ask you for money, you
          have to go. She's your child too.
               (beat)
          I just don't think it's fair that I
          have to sacrifice everything to
          your nothing.
               (beat)
          Sure. You can have her any time.
          Check or no check, you're her
          father. I'm just letting you know
          what I need to keep her going in
          all the activities I've enrolled
          her in.
               (beat)
          Yea, you do that.

Erica SLAMS the phone down.

## EXT. INDUSTRIAL AREA SOMEWHERE IN NJ - DAY

Chad is crossing the railroad tracks when an hysterical WHITE FEMALE lunges in front of his jeep.

Chad SCREECHES to a dead stop!

> WHITE FEMALE
> Help me, please! They took my car
> with my baby in it. Please, please!

> CHAD
> (adrenaline pumping)
> Who, where... who took your baby!?

> WHITE FEMALE
> (points behind Chad)
> Hurry! They're getting away.

Chad glances into his rearview mirror where he sees an expensive SUV struggling to beat traffic for a right turn at the corner stop sign.

> CHAD
> (to white female)
> Back up! Move out the way!

Chad throws the jeep in reverse, then turns the jeep around quickly with SQUEALING tires.

Chad speeds up the block, and cuts the SUV off just as it turns the corner, shocking the shit out the masked-driver and his two accomplices.

Chad bolts from the jeep and charges toward the driver. The Driver points a pistol and yanks off his mask, revealing himself -- it's Buddy #1.

> BUDDY #1
> (furious)
> What the fuck you doing, man?!

> CHAD
> (shocked)
> Oh, c'mon. Don't do this. Give me
> the baby, and drive off.

> BUDDY #1
> (to Buddy # 3; in back)
> Give him the fucking baby!
> (to chad)
> You really have changed. You a
> fucking crime stopper now!?

Chad takes the baby securely and steps back, still in shock, as his childhood buddies SQUEAL off.

Chad returns to scene where the mother is still in hysterics talking to police officers.

Chad gives the hysterical woman her baby in perfectly safe condition. The woman cradles her baby and drops to her knees.

> WHITE FEMALE
> (to Chad)
> Thank you, Stranger. Thank you so
> much. You put my life back
> together.

That moment, Phil Kearst breaks through a couple officers and rushes to the woman on her knees. He drops beside her and hugs her and the baby protectively.

> PHIL
> Are you okay, sweetie?

> WHITE FEMALE
> (in tears)
> Yes, Daddy, I'm fine.
> (points to Chad)
> This stranger chased down those
> bastards and brought little Joanne
> back to me.

Phil looks up. His face overwhelmed with confused expression between gratitude and guilt. He doesn't know what to say, and we know why.


## INT. ERICA'S FOYER - DAY

She opens the front door. What a delight -- it's Chad. He steps in.

Chad kisses her forehead. She hugs him and wraps his leg with hers -- she really likes him and it shows.

They kiss. They kiss again. Their faces lock. Chad's hand slides across her ass. She reaches back and lifts his hand up to her waist. She withdraws and rests her head against his chest.

> CHAD
> (worked up)
> Why'd you stop?

            ERICA
     (soft)
I cancelled my appointments. Had a
nice talk with Stephanie and Lisa
though.

            CHAD
Yeah?

            ERICA
Yeah. I want to go out tonight. I
need a drink.

            CHAD
What about Bria?

            ERICA
Tom picked her up from school, and
he's keeping her for the weekend.

            CHAD
Cool.

Erica takes him by the hand and guides him towards the living
room.


**INT. LIVING ROOM - DAY**

Erica takes a seat at her desk. She closes out her work and
tucks away her folder.

Chad sits on the sofa. She peeks at him while he anxiously
searches through his back-pack.

            ERICA
Take your hat off in my house.

He snatches off his cap and retrieves a script from his bag.

            CHAD
I've been revising my script, know
what I'm saying.

            ERICA
Good for you. Writing is your
passion. You should put more time
aside for it. And stop saying, "You
know what I'm saying."

            CHAD
What?

                    ERICA
I hate that. It makes people think
you can't complete a sentence.

                    CHAD
Saying, "You know what I'm saying?"

                    ERICA
          (annoyed)
Yes! You sound like those jerks at
the bar.


                    CHAD
          (shakes his head)
Jerks they are.

                    ERICA
I'm glad we agree on that.


                    CHAD
But, why would someone think I
can't complete a sentence, just
because I say, "You know what I'm
saying?"

                    ERICA
That's a good question, yet the
belief exists, so express yourself
fully.

                    CHAD
Okay, okay. Just read pages 61-63.

She reads a beat. Chad sits, anxiously awaiting feed back.
Erica completes all three pages and returns the script
without comment.

                    CHAD
          (c'mon)
What'd you think?


                    ERICA
I think it's good. I'm proud of
you.

                    CHAD
Is the story clearer now?

                    ERICA
Much. Each time I review it you
seem to have fluffed it some more.

                    CHAD
          Yeah?

                    ERICA
          Yeah. It's good. It sounds
          familiar, though. Like us, almost.

Erica stares at Chad. Her brow curiously wrinkled. Chad
pretends to be innocent.

                    CHAD
          What?

                    ERICA
            (suspect)
          You know how I feel about my
          privacy. I don't want my life open
          to the public.

                    CHAD
          It's not.

                    ERICA
          Okay. Then, It's really coming
          together.

He smiles, and tucks the script back in his bag.

                    CHAD
          You're my drive, baby-girl. I
          couldn't do it without you.

                    ERICA
          Don't give me the credit. It's in
          you, baby. That's what you're here
          to do, so do it. Impact the world
          with your literary talent.

He drops against the sofa pillows with a tired moan.

                    CHAD
          I wish my agent had the revised
          copy.

                    ERICA
          Is it too late?

                    CHAD
          Yea. She said some Dr. Looking to
          become an exec is interested in
          backing the movie.

                         ERICA
          Well, if they're not screaming re-
          write, don't stress. Apparently the
          copy you presented is good enough.

                         CHAD
          I want it to be a great -- not
          good. Great!

                         ERICA
          To reach that level you have to
          impose your will. It's never going
          to just come to you. You have to
          work for it.

He stares at Erica. She stares back a warmhearted beat. She
gets up from her seat and sits beside him.

                         ERICA
          Give me a hug. And kiss my cheek.

He obeys like a submissive puppy. She caresses his face. They
stare quietly and share smiles.

                         ERICA
               (soft)
          You're my best thing.

                         CHAD
          Thank you.

                         ERICA
               (peck his lips)
          How was your day?

                         CHAD
          You don't wanna know.

                         ERICA
          That crazy, huh?

                         CHAD
          And then some.

                         ERICA
          Did you eat?

                         CHAD
          Yeah.

                         ERICA
          What'd you have?

                    CHAD
Tuna.

                    ERICA
Did you drink any water today?

                    CHAD
Yeah.

                    ERICA
A little or a lot?

                    CHAD
        (laughs)
I guess a lot, baby. I drank a
liter this morning and one this
afternoon.

                    ERICA
        (she grins)
Don't laugh at my questions. I know
you don't eat properly, so I worry
about you.

                    CHAD
I'm okay, baby. Thank you. Did you
eat today?

She holds her stomach with a light frown.

                    ERICA
Yeah. I had a cheeseburger, but I
think it was a poor choice.

                    CHAD
got the runs?

                    ERICA
        (embarrassed)
No. I don't have the runs. But it
feels like I have a hunk of lead in
my stomach.

                    CHAD
Maybe you're pregnant.

                    ERICA
You wish. The burger was good
though. I tore it up.

He rubs her tummy. Erica holds her hand over his.

                    CHAD
          How's that?

                    ERICA
          Better. You're a big sweetie. You
          want anything to drink? I do. But
          there's nothing in the house.

**INT. SUPERMARKET - SODA AISLE - DAY**

Erica pushes her half-filled cart down the aisle. Chad
strolls beside her. She grabs a 12 pack of PEPSI.

                    ERICA
          I'm on call this week, so my work
          phone has been going berserk.

That instance her cell phone RINGS. Erica huffs with
annoyance. She gropes her purse.

                    ERICA
          I Talked it up.

Chad's busy in thought. He scribbles his ideas on a piece of
paper.

                    ERICA
              (to phone)
          Erica, may I help you?
              (beat)
          I'm the supervisor. Contact the
          care assistant.
              (beat)
          Right. It's Jessica's case.
              (beat)
          Yes, I'm familiar with it.
              (beat)
          Nothing serious. She's just usually
          hysterical -- probably knocked some
          things over. That sort of stuff.
              (beat)
          Okay. Bye.

She ends the call. Her eyes roll behind her head.

                    ERICA
          This on-call shit is really making
          me crazy.

                    CHAD
          Take it easy, babe.

> ERICA
> Earlier this woman calls saying her
> younger son was apoplectic and
> chasing his older brother through
> the woods with a knife. I'm like,
> "Call the police!" Hel-lo.

> CHAD
> (whatever, as he peeks at
> a passing female's ass)
> Right! What'd she call you for?

Erica catches him recklessly eyeballing the woman's ass.
Jealousy sweeps her face, and her stomach contracts like she
might puke.

She WHOPS Chad across the shoulder, but says nothing. Just
gives a hard, accusatory stare.

> CHAD
> What...? I heard you. I said,
> "Right. What'd she call you for?"

> ERICA
> (losing interest in
> talking)
> I don't know. Maybe she just needed
> a voice of reason. Let me pay for
> this and get out of here.

## INT. SUPERMARKET - CHECKOUT - DAY

As Erica and Chad approach the register, Erica runs into her
handsome colleague, Tony.

This is her chance to show Chad the pain of jealousy, so she
tests his level of affection with some over-the-top flirting.

> ERICA
> (smiling)
> Tony, hello.

Tony kisses her cheek, and she happily accepts. Chad is a
little displeased.

> TONY
> Good to see you, Erica.

> ERICA
> Same here. Yea, same here. So,
> when's the grand opening?

                    TONY
          we open for business next Friday.
          But I'm not leaving the agency.
          Not yet.

                    ERICA
          Alriiight!  I'm coming by for some
          discounts.

                    TONY
          Anytime.

                    ERICA
          Oh, Tony, this is Chad, my
          boyfriend.  Chad, this is Tony.
          You've heard about him.

Tony extends a handshake.  Chad isn't eager to meet.  He's
almost rude.  Tony waves good-bye to Erica.

                    TONY
          All right, Erica.  See you Monday.

                    ERICA
          Good night, Tony.

Erica is smiling, but Chad is flaring.

                    ERICA
          Tony is so cool.

                    CHAD
          Whatever.

                    ERICA
              (taunting)
          Don't be jealous, babe.  He's just
          a friend.

Erica places her items on the conveyer belt.

                    CHAD
          Friends get you all googily-eyed
          like that?  You sure you only know
          him from work?

                    ERICA
          Why the 21 questions?  I'm no
          different than you, other than I'm
          a woman.

Lisa finishes ringing her up. Chad's bagging-up.

> LISA
> $35.49.  Cash or credit?

> CHAD
> (to Erica)
> What does that mean?

> ERICA
> (to Lisa)
> Cash. Oh! I didn't even realize
> that was you. When did you start
> here?

> LISA
> A couple days ago. Stephanie's two
> registers down.

Erica waves proudly at Stephanie. Stephanie smiles and waves back.

> ERICA
> (to Chad)
> To answer your question. It means
> that I can appreciate a man and all
> of his physical attributes, the
> same as you do a woman.

Erica pays and receives her change. She and Chad head out.

**EXT. SUPERMARKET - PARKING LOT - DAY**

Chad is loading the groceries into the trunk.

> CHAD
> Oh, so you admit it -- you are
> digging him?

> ERICA
> I appreciate things about him.
> But, what's your beef?  You're the
> classic booty-watcher.
> (off Chad's look)
> Don't puff-up, babe. I'm not trying
> to argue. Just making a point.

They face each other across the roof of the car.

> CHAD
> Just making a point... and what's
> that point?

                    ERICA
              (carefully and delicately)
          Babe, Women have the same desires
          as men, but we behave differently
          because we must.

                    CHAD
              (sarcasim)
          Oh, so we're one at mind and heart,
          but we just behave differently,
          huh.


                    ERICA
          Right. Because if it was okay for
          women to pick up men the way men
          pick up women, the world we live in
          would be a different place.

                    CHAD
              (ego challenged)
          Ahhh. So, you're saying, you like
          men the way you think men like
          women, only you don't really act on
          it, because of the societal
          perception of female aggression?

                    ERICA
          Right. I'm not confused about it.
          Are you?

                    CHAD
          Suddenly, I don't feel so special.

                    ERICA
          Oh, but you are.

                    CHAD
          I think we need to talk about the
          level of emotional closeness that
          we're willing to accept in our
          cross-sex friends.

Erica's tickled by his jealousy.

## INT. ERICA'S LIVING ROOM - ON SOFA - DAY

Chad and Erica cuddle. Chad sips his PEPSI, then holds a
deadpan stare. Erica observes his lost regard.

She removes the can from his hand and places it on the coffee
table, then She pulls Chad closer. She looks him in the eyes
with a meddlesome glare.

                    ERICA
What's on your mind? You look like
you forgot where you put something.

                    CHAD
Really?

                    ERICA
Yea. Those handsome eyes seem lost.

                    CHAD
I want to be successful at writing,
babe, but I don't know.

                    ERICA
Are you doubting yourself?

                    CHAD
Yeah. A little bit. Sometimes I
worry that my best years are gone.

                    ERICA
Why? You have more life ahead of
you than you have behind you.

                    CHAD
I believe I lost the most
productive years of my life in
prison.

                    ERICA
That's probably, partly true. But
there's some people who've never
been locked away at all, yet are
far behind you. This is your second
chance. Use it wisely.

                    CHAD
I feel like... all the writer I
could have ever been, I should have
been already. And if I'm not it
within the next year... I'll
probably never be it... and that
worries me.

                    ERICA
Try to worry less and write more.

                    CHAD
That's an ideal way to look at it.
But let's think about the real
deal. No matter how much I write.
                    (MORE)

                    CHAD (cont'd)
an original story written by an
unknown, is a hard sell, you know
what I'm saying?

                    ERICA
Ugh! I hate that.

                    CHAD

What...?

                    ERICA
"You know what I'm saying." It's so
beneath you. Who have you been
around -- those jerks at the bar,
again?

                    CHAD
What would you like to me say when
I'm checking to see if you follow?
"Get my meaning," "Comprehend what
I'm throwing down?"  Which one?

                    ERICA
Anything beats "You know what I'm
saying."

                    CHAD
Ok. You win.

                    ERICA
Thank you. Besides, you have
someone interested in your work.
Give it a chance to develop.

                    CHAD
All I'm saying is, I have to hurry
up and become the person I want to
be, before it's too late.

                    ERICA
The promise of greatness is already
in you. Don't rush it. Slow and
steady wins the race.

                    CHAD
     (checks his watch)
I wanna' stop at the bank and see
if my loan was approved. Meet you
at Chakra's?

                    ERICA
It's only 2pm.

                         CHAD
          I have to, uh. I gotta make a stop.

Erica senses nervous deceit in his fumbling words, but she
doesn't want to pry -- she rescues him instead.

                         ERICA
          Your daughters?

                         CHAD
                (voila)
          Yeah.  Promised the girls I'd
          pick'em up and take'em by the mall.

                         ERICA
                (she knows better)
          Okay.  Chakra's, eight'0 clock.
          Don't be late.


**EXT. PARK - NIGHT**

As we TRACK across the park we notice a woman leaning against
the tree. As we get closer we see that her shirt is open to
expose one of her breast, which rest against the rigid bark.


ON WOMAN

JANICE HARRIS, late twenties, long hair, stylish nightlife
clothes. Her eyes are rolling in ecstacy. A hand caresses her
breast from behind. We follow the hand and see Chad crouched
behind her, grinding her ass.

Chad raises her skirt and flaps it over the small of her
back. He rises up behind her and penetrates slowly. Her neck
arches. Her eyes half closed.

Chad presses his hand against the small of her back, slightly
bending her more. She rotates her pelvis gently against his
thrusting. It gets good to him.

Janice MOANS in delight as Chad penetrates harder. He YANKS
Janice by the waist as he thrust deeply. Janice WHIMPERS as
she enjoys him bouncing against her ass.

                         JANICE
                (she pants)
          Pull my hair.

Chad grabs a head full of hair, pulling Janice's head back.

                    JANICE
          Ugh. Not too hard.

His grip loosens.

                    JANICE
                 (turned on)
          Yeah, like that.

Thirty feet away, through the thick of bushes, we get the
impression someone else is in the park. An unseen visitor
observing Janice and Chad.


BACK TO SCENE

Chad's stroke speeds up. He pounds harder and harder. We hear
the SMACKING of their sweaty flesh.

Janice's mouth falls open. Her eyes stretch wide, then roll
behind her head.

Chad's rabbit-stroking slows down as he lets out a GRUNT of
pleasure. He gives one final thrust and holds it as he
climaxes.

Janice fights to hold back her screams of ecstacy as she
arches her back and pokes out her ass to take all that he's
giving her.

Then, Janice climaxes too. Her head drops, and her legs shake
involuntarily as she takes a deep breath.


BUSHES

A hand moves into OUR FRAME and pulls back some vines for a
clearer view. Leaves CRUNCH and a twigs POP.

                    CHAD
                 (out of breath)
          You hear something?

                    JANICE
                 (passive)
          No. You try'na scare me? Wow that
          was great. I needed that.

Chad pulls his body back, adjusting his pants. She buttons
her shirt.

Janice turns and faces Chad. She puts her arms on his
shoulders and pecks his lips.

                    CHAD
          You are amazing.

                    JANICE
          This is just... this is so crazy.
          We're supposed to be friends.

                    VOICE (O.S.)
          Okay, show's over.

Two teens scurry from the thorn bushes GIGGLING and SLAPPING
fives.

Horrified by the voice out of nowhere and the sound of
scuffling feet, Janice turns with her hand across her chest.
She sighs in relief -- it's an OFFICER.

                    JANICE
          Oh, you scared me.

                    OFFICER
          Sorry, mam. Didn't mean to scare
          you.

                    CHAD
          Everything okay?

                    OFFICER
          Yeah, if you'd guys just get a
          room. You're drawing an under age
          audience.

                    JANICE
          We're leaving now, officer.

                    OFFICER
          Thank you.


EXT. CHAKRA'S - NIGHT

Patrons crowd at the entrance. Many conversations are going
at once.

Erica is on her toes,  peering over the head and shoulders of
the crowd, searching for Chad. Her face shows the fear and
disappointment of being stood-up.

Chad's neck swivels this way, then that. He's searching for
Erica. He appears disappointed as well.

Chad's about to leave when he takes a final glance over his
right shoulder and sees Erica weaving through the crowd.

He's swept with excitement, and he motions eagerly for her with waving arms.

Erica can tell he's not upset, and She's so relieved and smiles with increased excitement.

They finally reach other. Erica holds his face as she pecks his lips again and again. She's so delighted.

                    ERICA
          Sorry I'm late, babe. You know how
          us women do.

                    CHAD (V.O.)
          I thought she had gone because I
          was late, at which point I felt
          guilty for being with Janice, but
          realizing she was unaware of my
          lateness, my fear to create a
          believable excuse disappeared. I
          guess it just went favorably for
          the sake of her heart rather than
          my bullshit.

                    ERICA
          How long you been waiting?

                    CHAD
          Don't worry about it.

                    ERICA
             (pecks him again)
          Thank you, Babe for not being
          angry.

Chad gives her a once over, and he's impressed with her look.

                    CHAD
          Wow! You look Awesome.

                    ERICA
             (seductively)
          Did you forget? I can be many
          things, and sexy is one of them.
          Better act right, or you're gunnuh
          miss this.

                    CHAD
          That is borderline sexy and
          crossing over to-

                    ERICA
Hold that thought. Appreciate the
hooch in me. You'll never see me
Butt naked in the street, or
sliding down a pole at a club, but
sometimes I feel frisky, and like
to command attention.

                    CHAD
You're doing a great job of it
tonight.

                    ERICA
          (grinning)
Grow old with me, babe, and the
best is yet to come.

## INT. CHAKRA'S - NIGHT

A stylish lounge dimly lit, mainly through the aid of
candles. Couples and friends cram the joint.

Chad and Erica sip while seated at a window table for two.

                    ERICA
How'd the loan interview go?

                    CHAD
They denied me.

                    ERICA
What did you expect? You're not
working.  How long have I been
telling you to get a job?  Continue
writing, but get a job until your
big break.

                    CHAD
I went on four interviews this past
week. I just can't get a leg up
with my background.  But being
unemployed isn't I was denied. They
specified I haven't occupied
residency at one address for at
least three years.
          (sips drink)
But the Arab beside me who just got
in the country five minutes ago,
got approved for a million dollars.
Guess he's opening up some discount
gas station.

> ERICA
> Hey! Not nice. What if they accused
> you of wanting the loan to open a
> rap studio, or buy some chrome rims
> for your new SUV?

> CHAD
> You're right. I take it back. I
> just don't get it.

> ERICA
> It's called disenfranchise. It's
> when you favor some over others and
> play the ends against the middle.
> You give those from another country
> the opportunity to move ahead, and
> leave those already here, behind.
> Before you know it, America's going
> to fill with people who aren't
> really about what this country is
> about. These other groups are going
> to have certain sympathies for
> their homeland, and their goals
> will be to reach out to them. Then,
> before long, we'll have a president
> named Habib -- that's the direction
> of America.

## INT. ERICA'S FOYER - NIGHT

Erica closes the door and locks it. We follow her and Chad to
the living room sofa where they sit.

They are giddy, and look like they had plenty to drink.

> ERICA
> I had a really nice time tonight.
> Thank you, baby.

> CHAD
> My pleasure.

Erica traces his lips with her finger. She begins kissing him
with lust and passion, and then she gently pulls away.

> ERICA
> Who knew?

> CHAD
> What...?

                    ERICA
          That the day we met would turn into
          this?


**FLASHBACK**


**EXT. CINEPLEX - PARKING LOT - DAY**

Chad steps out the Jeep. TERELL, a chubby eight year old
steps out of the passenger side.

Chad notices an attractive, woman crossing the lot. It's
Erica.

                    CHAD
          Wait, Relli. Don't go yet.

                    RELLI
          We goin' miss the beginning.

                    CHAD
               (he peeks at his watch)
          We got time.

Relli notices Chad gawking Erica.

                    RELLI
          You sweatin' that girl.

                    CHAD
               (slightly annoyed)
          Chill out, Relli.

Erica crosses Chad's path about ten feet away.

                    CHAD
               (to Erica)
          Hello.

Erica stops and turns with her hand over her brow to shield
her eyes from the sun.

                    ERICA
          Hello.

                    CHAD
          Uh, you have a second -- is it okay
          if I approach?

                    ERICA
          Sure.

Chad turns and holds up one finger to Relli, Then struts
toward Erica. Chad extends his hand, they shake.

                    CHAD
          Hi, I'm Chad. May I ask your name?

                    ERICA
          I'm Erica.

                    CHAD
          Pleased to meet you.

                    ERICA
          Likewise.

Chad looks over to Relli who's sitting Indian style on the
ground. Chad motions for him to stand.

                    ERICA
          Is that your son?

                    CHAD
          No. That's Relli, my friend's son.
          I picked him up from school to
          treat him to Big Mama's House.

                    ERICA
          Awwww. How nice.

                    CHAD
            (curious)
          Are you alone.

                    ERICA
          Yea. I do this a lot.

                    CHAD
            (looking back at Relli)
          Well, I don't want him to miss the
          beginning.
            (back to Erica)
          but I don't want to rush this
          opportunity either.

                    ERICA
          I understand completely. Will
          anyone be upset if I give you my
          number?

                    CHAD
          No! No one I can think of.

                    ERICA
          Let me get a pen. Follow me, I'm
          just right here.

Erica opens the driver door. Chad notices the car is a bit
messy. He observes a car seat in the back.

                    ERICA
          Excuse my mess. I don't always have
          the energy to keep the car clean.

                    CHAD
          I'm not judging.

                    ERICA
          Good.

Erica bends into the car searching for a pen. Chad gazes at
her round ass. As She backs out of the car, Chad snaps out of
his lusty trance.

                    CHAD
          You're a mom, huh?

                    ERICA
          Yeah. I have a two year old.

Erica holds up a pen and a small piece of paper.

                    ERICA
          Now, you're sure no one will be
          angry with me for giving you my
          number?

                    CHAD
          I'm so sure.

                    ERICA
          Okay.

Erica writes down her number on the paper and passes it to
Chad.

                    CHAD
          Thank you, Erica. I feel lucky to
          have met you. You'll hear from me
          soon.

                    ERICA
          We'll see. Enjoy the movie.

Chad motions for Relli, and they head for the ticket booth as Erica looks on. Chad gives a final wave to Erica. She waves back.

                    ERICA
          It's a funny movie, Relli. You'll
          like it.

                    RELLI
               (to Chad)
          How's she know my name.

Chad affectionately pushes the back of Relli's head.


**BACK TO SCENE**

                    ERICA
               (smiling)
          You were such a gentlemen. And you
          still have that beat-up jeep.

                    CHAD
          Oh, that hurts.

                    ERICA
          No seriously, Babe. Do you know how
          long ago that was? Bria was only
          two then. She's four now.

                    CHAD
          Wow. Yea, it's two years and some
          change now.

                    ERICA
          You've been home how long -- three
          years -- and we've been together
          over two? Babe, you know I want to
          get married, and I want another
          kid, so hurry up and get it
          together. I don't care if it's
          Shoprite, McDonald's or what. But
          you have to get a job. We need to
          start sharing or resources and
          behaving more like a real couple.

                    CHAD
          Okay, baby.

                    ERICA
          I mean it.

                         CHAD
                    Okay.

They kiss. Chad's hand begins to roam across her back and
over her ass.

Erica continues kissing him as she gently removes his hand.
His eyes roll with frustration.

                         CHAD
                    Why do you always move my hand
                    away?

                         ERICA
                         (pecks his lips)
                    You have such nice eyes, but you
                    don't wear them well when you're
                    acting a fool.

                         CHAD
                         (as he looks away)
                    Whatever.

                         ERICA
                    Look at me. Look at me, Chad.

He glares from the corner of his eye.

                         ERICA
                         (trying to jolly him up)
                    See what I mean. Your eyes just
                    aren't as nice when you're cutting
                    them left to right like that.

He flags her off.

                         ERICA
                    Is this the start of a hissy-fit?

                         CHAD
                    No. It's not a hissy-fit, I'm just
                    saying.

                         ERICA
                    You're saying what? Is it okay for
                    me to kiss you without it going any
                    further? Why must you throw a tizzy
                    when I say no to sex?

                         CHAD
                    I mean, c'mon. Are we ever gunnuh
                    do it again?

She holds him by the hands and looks him in the eye with
concern.

                    ERICA
          I kissed you because I couldn't
          resist. But, I didn't mean to open
          you up for something else, just to
          shut you down.

Chad snatches his back-pack. He gets up and heads for the
door. Erica remains on the sofa.

                    CHAD
          I'll see you later.

                    ERICA
          See how you are? You're going to go
          -- just like that?

                    CHAD
          I have something to do.

                    ERICA
          Okay. I won't hold you up. You
          coming to church with me Sunday?

He remains silent for a beat. She gets up and barricades him
with her body.

                    CHAD
          I don't know.
               (beat)
          Excuse me.

                    ERICA
          No. You're not going to run just
          because I won't give you some.

                    CHAD
          Excuse me. I have to go.

                    ERICA
          No. You're not going. Sit down. I
          want to talk to you.

Chad huffs heavily, but he really doesn't want to leave. He
sits back on the sofa. Erica sits down beside him.

                    ERICA
          Baby, let me give you a clue,
          because apparently, you don't have
          one.

                    CHAD
          No...?

                    ERICA
          Our missed-match of sexual desires
          shouldn't be a real issue.
               (beat)
          Here's the issue. Can you be my
          man, and <u>can</u> you be what I need, or
          not? Think about that for a while
          and get back to me.

He pops to his feet. He paces angrily.

                    CHAD
          I'm trying to be your man and what
          you need, but you won't let me.

                    ERICA
          No you're not. You're trying to
          figure out how you can get some.
          Being what I need is more than
          that.

                    CHAD
          Maybe it's Tony you want?

                    ERICA
          Baby, sit down.

                    CHAD
          Why can't I stand?

                    ERICA
          Because you're pouncing around like
          a wild man, and it's making me
          uncomfortable.

                    CHAD
          Making you uncomfortable? Why,
          because I'm an ex-con?

Erica tries to maintain her firmness, but can't resist
chuckling at his silly comment.

                    ERICA
          No, baby. It doesn't bother me at
          all that you're an ex-con. If that
          were the case you wouldn't be a
          part of my life. Don't be so
          defensive.

                    CHAD
              (as he sits)
          Better?


                    ERICA
          Much better. I'm a woman who's been
          physically abused by a man before.
          That's why I get nervous when an
          angry man prances over me.

                    CHAD
          Sorry.


                    ERICA
          It's okay, Baby. Just relax a bit.
          Let me go change into my night
          clothes. When I get back, finish
          telling me what's on your mind.

Chad throws his head to the back of the sofa and takes a deep
breath. Erica rubs his forehead.


**EXT. URBAN STREETS - DOWNTOWN NIGHT**

Yvonne and her home girls march through the pedestrian
walkway, but the light is green, and they don't care.

Cars SCREECH to a halt to avoid hitting them. Angry drivers
spew irate comments, but the girls never miss a beat --
they're stepping with purpose.

**INT. MCDONALD'S RESTAURANT - DOWNTOWN - NIGHT**

It prepares for closing. The custodial team is mopping up and
wiping down tables. Stephanie and Lisa are finishing off
combination meals.

                    LISA
          I guess I'll tell them when I get
          back. You coming with me?

                    STEPHANIE
          Yeah, I'll come.

                    LISA
          You should spend the night. Can
          you?

                    STEPHANIE
              (she shrugs)
          I guess so. I'll be sanctioned
          though.
                    (MORE)

                    STEPHANIE (cont'd)
          And I probably won't be able to
          come back out for two weekends.

                    LISA
          Don't get an any trouble.

The girls share a look that says they need each other.

                    STEPHANIE
          Forget that girls home. I'm staying
          with you.

                    LISA
          Yay!

                    STEPHANIE
          You're so silly.

Lisa looks toward the door and sees Yvonne and her home girls
standing out front. Yvonne doesn't look happy.

                    LISA
               (worried)
          Is that Yvonne?

Stephanie quickly turns to see. Worry sweeps her face.

                    STEPHANIE
          Yeah, that's her.


**EXT. MCDONALD'S - NIGHT**

Lisa and Stephanie exit McDonald's. Yvonne is hyper. Her home
girls try to calm her down.

                    YVONNE
               (to her friends)
          No, this bitch is wrong! She knew
          Kenneth was my man. She knew I
          already had a baby with him, and
          her trifling ass is going to go and
          get pregnant by him! This bitch is
          mine.

Lisa and Stephanie try to walk away, but Yvonne's friend,
AMANDA, a total instigator, discreetly passes a Yvonne a
DAGGER.

Stephanie tries to confront Yvonne with ration, but Yvonne's
goons SHOVE her back.

Stephanie's edge start to show, and she's ready for whatever!

Yvonne steps toward Lisa. Stephanie steps in between and
PUSHES Yvonne back.

                    STEPHANIE
          Don't let these wiry limbs fool
          you.

                    YVONNE
          This ain't got nothing to do with
          you, Stephanie.

Yvonne SWINGS over Stephanie's shoulder, and nearly hits Lisa
in the face. Stephanie pushes her again -- harder this time.

                    YVONNE
          Ahma kill that fucking baby, and
          that bitch!

Yvonne tries to kick Lisa in the stomach, but Stephanie
SNATCHES her leg and TOSSES her to the ground. Yvonne SPRINGS
up and Stephanie BOXES her in the nose, knocking her back to
the ground.

                    STEPHANIE
          She's pregnant, Yvonne! You wanna
          fight so bad, fight me!

Violent beat. The home girls assemble. Stephanie is enraged,
but Lisa is fearful, especially for the baby.

We see a shiny steel dagger being secretly passed from hand
to hand.

                    LISA
          C'mon, Stephanie. Lets just go.

Lisa and Stephanie try backing away, but the goons attack
Stephanie.

Lisa jumps in and tries to pull Stephanie free from the
ruckus.

Yvonne squirms out of the confusion and crawls to her feet.
She draws the dagger -- she thinks a beat... then... spurred
by rage, grief, and jealousy she charges toward Lisa.

Yvonne raise the dagger high over her head, then SPLAT!
Yvonne JAMS the dagger into Lisa's side.

Lisa STUMBLES back. She loses her breath -- her mouth gapes.
Blood stains her clothes.

Lisa can't believe it -- her eyes bugged with fright. You can tell by the look on her face, she knows she's dying -- quickly!

All the girls are in shock, but none more than Stephanie, whom is in tears and panic.

Stephanie rushes to Lisa's aid, bearing her weight to the ground. Blood stains the pavement beneath her.

The home girls back off -- they're scared!

Yvonne's bloodied hand trembles. A blood droplet from  dagger SPLASHES to the ground.

Yvonne looks almost psycho -- crossed between cavalier for putting in work, and scared for the outcome.

Yvonne and the home girls zip off. They fork themselves over a nearby fence, losing balance as they hit the other side. They hustle to their feet and disappear into the dark of the night.

Stephanie and Lisa are left helpless. McDonald's workers rush out to assist the best way they can.

Police FLASHERS are reflecting of off buildings and ambulance sirens can be heard in the near distance.


**INT. ERICA'S LIVING ROOM - NIGHT**

Erica returns in her sky-blue, childlike pajamas, decorated with clouds. She sits down beside Chad. He's in deep thought.

                    ERICA
          What's on your mind?

                    CHAD
          So, it's Tony, huh?

                    ERICA
          I'm lost -- it's Tony what?

                    CHAD
          Tony! The guy from work who you
          find so cool?

                    ERICA
          Yeah, he's cool. Cool like
          interesting.

                    CHAD
What does he do for your great
appreciation of men?

                    ERICA
Is that what you do with the things
I tell you -- wait for an
opportunity to use my words against
me? What you're doing is really not
conducive to this situation.

                    CHAD
But you do like men, and you do
find Tony interesting, right?

                    ERICA
I appreciate men, and I'll be the
first to admit it. But what I find
interesting in Tony has nothing to
do with sex. I don't know why you
insist on correlating the two. I
find interesting in Tony what I
find interesting in you.

                    CHAD
          (not feeling any resolve)
Yeah, what is that?

                    ERICA
A young man with direction and
ambition. One who wants more out of
life.
          (beat)
What I find particularly
interesting in Tony is his
entrepreneurial drive.

                    CHAD
          (jealous)
Okay, you said a mouthful about
him. What do you find interesting
in me?

Erica smiles and kisses his cheek.

                    ERICA
Besides being so damn fine -- I
think you're one of the smartest
men I know. You're the only writer
I know -- and last, but not least,
I love your self-consciousness of
your place in this world. That's
what I find interesting about you.

He humbles himself. His demeanor apologetic. He leans his
head on Erica's shoulder like a tamed little house-cat.

                    CHAD
          I've never in my life met a woman
          like you. I guess that's why I get
          so jealous when you deny me. Then I
          worry that there's someone else.

                    ERICA
          There's no one else. And I don't
          enjoy denying you. That's what I'm
          trying to clue you in on.

                    CHAD
          I just don't know what to think at
          times. I'm sure I don't deserve you
          anyway.

                    ERICA
          Don't be silly. A part of my
          frustration is having to hard-line
          you, when in fact, I really want
          some too.

                    CHAD
          I just don't know what to say or
          do. You make me feel like my
          attempts to show my love don't
          really count for much.

                    ERICA
          My goal isn't to make you feel
          inadequate about your love for me.
          I just need to be in the right
          space for sex, and I am so not
          there right now. Baby, if you want
          this, it's here for you, but you
          have to know how to warm it up.

                    CHAD
          I'm ready to earn my wings.

                    ERICA
          Earn your wings?

                    CHAD
          You know...

                    ERICA
             (snickers childishly)
          You don't know how much I would
          like that.
             (MORE)

                    ERICA (cont'd)
It's just I have to be sure you
appreciate this before I give it
away, again.

                    CHAD
          (whirling his tongue)
I appreciate it.

                    ERICA
          (grinning)
Slow down, babe. I love the fact
that you want me that way, but
that's not what I mean when I say
warm it up.

Erica holds her heart with both hands.

                    ERICA
You can find out about me. See how
Erica's doing? Rub my feet, because
you know I've been on them all day
Rub my back because you know it
aches. Ask me how I'm feeling. Make
sure I'm okay. And come to my house
with something in your hand -- a
flower, chocolates, a card.
Something to let me know you're
thinking about Erica. Don't let the
romance slip away, Babe.

                    CHAD
          (ashamed)
I understand.

Erica rubs his back and glares at him with adoring eyes.

                    ERICA
Just think, babe. You have all my
numbers, you know where I work and
where I live. But I don't know
anything about you. You say you
live in a rooming house, but you
won't let me visit you there, and
you have no cell phone. I can't
even reach you if I needed to. But
I don't sweat you. My house of
doubt is really big, but I don't
make any demands about where you
really go when you leave here. So,
if you want this every time you
want it, then you're gunnuh have to
open up your life to me a little
bit more.

                         CHAD
                    (put in his place)
               I'm sorry, baby.


                         ERICA
               It's my fault too, for letting it
               go down like this. But things have
               to change soon. It's been two
               years, Chad.

                         CHAD
               I'll be more considerate.

                         ERICA
               That's all I ask.

Chad goes to the desk and sits a beat. He starts writing.

Erica gets up and stands over his shoulder as he jots down
his ideas. Erica tries to snatch the paper, but Chad pulls
away just in time.

                         CHAD
               What're you doing?


                         ERICA
               What are you doing?


                         CHAD
               I'm writing.


                         ERICA
               You're writing my words.


                         CHAD
               I'm writing our conversation.


                         ERICA
               Why?


                         CHAD
               You said some interesting things.
               You have a unique view on life, so
               I thought to create a character
               just like you, for my script.

Erica reaches for the paper again, but Chad secures it.

                         ERICA
               Give it to me.


                         CHAD
               Why -- what's the big deal?

                    ERICA
          I don't want to be a character in
          your script. I don't want my words
          and feelings about us, open to the
          public. Can I have my privacy?

                    CHAD
          Yeah, you have your privacy.

                    ERICA
          Then give me my words.

Beat. He submissively hands her the paper.

                    ERICA
          Thank you.

She rips the paper and sprinkles the litter into a tiny trash
bucket beside her computer desk.

                    ERICA
          You should get a laptop, anyway.

                    CHAD
          I'm working on it.

                    ERICA
          We had a fun night. How about
          ending it on a good note?

                    CHAD
          Sure.

                    ERICA
          You staying over, or are you going?

                    CHAD
          Staying I guess.

                    ERICA
               (takes him by the hand)
          Let's get some sleep.


## INT. BANK'S LIVING ROOM - NIGHT

Woodrow's geared in his army field jacket, jumper boots, and
a combat helmet.

He marches around drunk and wild-eyed. He swigs vodka from
his service flagon.

Rosina conceals a small canister of pepper spray.

                    ROSINA
          This is goin' be for your own good,
          Woodrow.

Woodrow drops to one knee. He operates his portable radio as
if it were a tactical communications system. He behaves like
he's in the trenches, and he rants engagement commands.

                    ROSINA
                  (troubled)
          Woodrow, please stop drinking and
          sit down. Talk to me, Woodrow.

He snaps! And Rosina becomes an enemy of the Gulf War. He
surges toward her.

                    WOODROW
          I told yo' big ass don't mess wit'
          me.

She stands steady, in fright. When he gets close, Rosina
SQUIRTS him frantically with the pepper spray.

He stumbles in agony. His arm dropping mid-swing. His flagon
CLINK-CLANKS to the floor. Vodka spills.

                    WOODROW
          Ough!

                    ROSINA
                  (pained emotionally)
          You stupid drunk! You ain't gone be
          satisfied to that alcohol kills
          you!

                    WOODROW
          Whut'chu do to me? Whut the hell
          you put in my eyes?

He swats his face vigorously with both hands, desperate to
clear the fiery substance.

He staggers wildly into wall. He lifts his T-shirt to his
face, frantically wiping his eyes. He examines the reddish-
orange substance on his shirt and blinks wildly.

                    WOODROW
          You threw hot sauce in my eyes!

                    ROSINA
          That ain't no hot sauce, stupid!

She bluffs to strike him.

>                    ROSINA
>      Now, get your drunk ass up stairs
>      and go to sleep. Alcohol's got your
>      brain so messed up. We can't even
>      get along and to our child.

Their fight is interrupted by a KNOCK on the door. We follow
Rosina to the door. She opens it. It's two officers -- their
faces regretful.

>                    ROSINA
>      Everything's under control. My
>      husband's drunk and having
>      flashbacks. I sent him to bed now.

>                    OFFICER #2
>      Ma'm, that's not what we're here
>      for.

>                    ROSINA
>              (worried)
>      Well, then. How can I help you?

>                    OFFICER #1
>      Are you the biological parent, or
>      the legal guardian of Lisa Banks?

>                    ROSINA
>              (panicked)
>      Yes. Yes, I am. What is it...? Is
>      there a problem?

## INT. ERICA'S KITCHEN - NEXT MORNING

Erica lifts her shade to welcome in the sunshine. Chad enters
the kitchen wearing sweats and a undersized, POWER PUFF GIRL,
T-shirt.

>                    ERICA
>      Morning, babe.

>                    CHAD
>      Morning. You need to work on your T-
>      shirt game.

>                    ERICA
>              (searches cabinet)
>      I think it looks cute on you.
>              (she pauses)
>      I can't believe it. I forgot to buy
>      water and paper towels. Will you go
>      to the store for me -- please?

                    CHAD
          I gotta' make a few runs.

                    ERICA
          Okay, don't worry about it. Coming
          back later?

                    CHAD
          Of course. Round noonish.

                    ERICA
               (smiling)
          Okay.

She kisses his cheek.


## INT. CONVENIENCE STORE - CHECK-OUT - MORNING

Erica drops her paper towels and water on the counter.
Suddenly, her eyes spring wide open.

She is as startled as she could ever be -- she releases a
stressful sigh. Tears begin dripping -- her hand covers her
mouth, but we don't know what she's looking at.

Erica's hand reaches for the news wrack. We stare at the
front page with her.

Lisa's photo takes up the picture box. HEADLINES: **ROMANTIC
JEALOUSY; PREGNANT TEEN STABBED TO DEATH.**


## INT. PANCAKE HOUSE - MORNING

The house is full. Customers wait for tables to clear. Chad,
Lana, and the kids are seated in a rear booth eating their
meals.

                    LANA
          These our the moments I really
          enjoy about our relationship. You
          may be very busy -- with what, I
          have no clue. I guess your writing.
          But you're really a good man, with
          a good heart. You have a lot of
          growing to do, but You've come a
          long way, and I'm proud of you.

Chad strains an appreciative grin.

                    CHAD (V.O.)
All the people in my life seem to
give me more credit than I deserve,
but it never hurts more than when
Lana does it. I owe her and my
children so much of me, yet I give
them so little.

                    JOY
Daddy, are you going out again,
tonight?

                    CHAD
I'll be in early. I just have
something to do this afternoon.

                    LANA
I thought we were going to do
something -- as a family?

                    CHAD
We are, baby. Don't worry.


**INT. JANICE'S APARTMENT - KITCHEN - AFTERNOON**

A stylish one bed room apartment. Janice is in her gown
scrambling eggs while holding the phone to her ear with her
shoulder.

                    JANICE
                 (to phone)
I understand, Chad, but all I ask
for is a phone call. Just a little
courtesy to say you're stuck.
Otherwise I'm left to believe there
must be someone else.
                 (beat)
What time?

                    JANICE
                 (breaks a smile; to phone)
You better not mess up.


**INT. ERICA'S LIVING ROOM - NOON**

Erica is curled up in her couch. She is pained. Her face
tired from crying. Used tissues lay carelessly about.

The phone RINGS. She peeks at the I.D. It's Tom. She'd rather
not answer, but it may concern Bria.

                    ERICA
            (to phone; sad)
    What's the problem, Tom?
            (beat)
    Everything is in her bag. Did you
    ask her?
            (beat)
    She knows where it is. Let me speak
    to her.
            (beat)
    Hi, sweetie. I miss you.
            (beat)
    Show dad where your medicine is,
    okay -- good girl, now put daddy
    on.
            (beat)
    Okay, see you.
            (beat)
    I'm not sure.
            (beat)
    Yes, I'm home alone. Why are you
    asking me my business?
            (beat)
    Tom, I'm not even going to
    entertain this conversation. I'm
    going to lay down now. Good night.


**INT. PRISON SHOWER ROOM - DAY**

Prisoners are showering. Most are built like athletes and
have jailhouse tats.

Chad enters, but for some odd reason he appears insecure.
Vapors of steam obscure or view.

                    CHAD (V.O.)
    That was pretty much a problem for
    me. I've always felt uncomfortable
    being naked around other naked men.
    Their thick flesh dangling between
    their legs. But mine, just not as
    fleshy.


**INT. DR LEVIN'S OFFICE - DAY**

We join Chad and his macho issues. He's lying on a couch,
recounting his woes to DR. Levin.

                    CHAD
    My size insecurities made feel
    isolated. Less manly.

                    DR. LEVIN
          What was a woman's reaction to your
          size, and how did that effect you?

                    CHAD
           Well, I've never had a woman say,
          "Wow! Your huge." But, I have
          heard, "Make it bigger." What a
          number that did on my ego. I get
          afraid that, eventually a woman's
          going to leave me for a more
          fulfilling sex partner. I mean,
          even if they love me, and they show
          their love for me, still, I harbor
          this fear of being sexually
          inadequate.

                    DR. LEVIN
          Perhaps, the same reasons you went
          to prison for violent crimes, is
          the same reasons you have many
          women. You're chasing a feeling of
          manliness within.

                    CHAD
          maybe, Doc. I mean, when a woman
          yells, "deeper. Harder. Hit me." I
          get nervous. I'm already giving it
          my best. I'm just not endowed for
          the jack-hammer thrust sorta' deal.
          The whole thing makes me feel
          insignificant most times.

                    DR. LEVIN
          This problem you have, I'm sure
          it's deep rooted. Next session I
          want you to tell me about your dad.
          What he was like -- what you
          thought of him?


**INT. JANICE'S APARTMENT - BEDROOM - DAY**

Janice is looking hot in her red lingerie. She turns up the
stereo. She's listening to <u>Rock Your Baby</u>, by George Mcrae.

There's a SOFT KNOCK. Janice goes to the door. She cracks it
and peeks, then swings it open. It's Chad.

                    JANICE
          Come in, baby.

He steps in, taking no notice of her sexy sleep wear. She is
annoyed by his failure to be impressed with her.

                    CHAD
          We have to talk.

                    JANICE
          Sounds important. Didn't know I
          mattered so much.

                    CHAD
          I have to stop seeing you.

                    JANICE
          Before you ride off on your horse,
          I have something to talk to you
          about.

                    CHAD
          Janice, you're a great girl. But
          I'm not being fair to you,
          myself... and... I'm just confused.
               (off her look)
          Don't tell me you're pregnant.

                    JANICE
          Don't look at me like it's my
          fault. I always say, "Babe, get a
          condom." And you always say, "I'll
          pull out," but you never do.
               (beat)
          And I'm keeping it. I won't have a
          fourth abortion.

Chad is disappointed, but Janice is final in her decision. He
goes for the front door.

                    CHAD
          I gotta run.

                    JANICE
               (irked)
          That's what you do best.


**INT. CHAD'S LIVING ROOM - NIGHT**

Lana and the girls are having ice cream over a movie. Chad Jr
is sleeping across Diana's lap.

Lana surprises the girls and passes them her e.p.t. results.

                    JOY
                (excited)
        Uh!

She passes it to Sabrina.

                    SABRINA
        Does daddy know...?

                    LANA
        I'm going to tell him when he comes
        home. He'll be in early tonight.

                    DIANA
        I hope it's another boy.

                    JOY
        Yeah. I want a another brother.

                    LANA
        I hope it's a boy, too.


## INT. CHAD'S LIVING ROOM - WEE HOURS

It's dark except a glow from the floor TV. The girls are
sleeping wildly across the couch and floor. The television
plays at a mild volume.


## INT. KITCHEN - WEE HOURS

An ice bucket sits on an elegant three-legged stand. A
depression is hollowed in the ice -- where the champaign
bottle is missing.

The table is romantically set for two, but the now cold
Plates of food and the dissipating bubbles in the Champagne
glasses make a mockery of Lana's attempt for a romantic night
with Chad.

We see a note. CLOSE ON NOTE as we read--

                    LANA (V.O.)
        "You said you'd be in early
        tonight. I was foolishly
        optimistic. Really, I knew better,
        but I wanted to believe different.
        Whoever she is, I hope she's worth
        it. I miss you. The kids miss you.
        Love always, Lana."

**INT. MASTER BEDROOM - WEE HOURS**

Chad Jr. is asleep on the bed. Lana is dancing in the mirror. The near empty bottle of Champagne rests on her vanity set. She's sad, buzzed, and hurt. It's obvious she's been crying.

Lana is singing along and moving to the Diana Ross hit, Upsidedown.

>                    LANA
>           (singing)
> *Instinctively you give to me*
> *The love that I need*
> *I cher-rish the moments with you*
> *Respectfully I say to thee*
> *I'm aware that you're cheating*
> *But no one makes me feel like you*
> *do.*
>           (chorus)
> *I know you got charm and appeal*
> *You always play the field*
> *I'm cra-zy to think you're all mine*
> *As long as the sun continues to*
> *shine*
> *There's a place in my heart for you*
> *That's the bottom line.*
>           (chorus)

**INT. ERICA'S FOYER - WEE HOURS**

Erica's covered in her Robe and extremely tired. She opens the door to let Chad in. He enters with great enthusiasm.

>                    ERICA
>           (angry)
> You made it -- finally?

>                    CHAD
> Sorry, Baby.

>                    ERICA
>           (angry as hell)
> It's okay. You got a better offer.

>                    CHAD
>           (regretful)
> Baby.

>                    ERICA
> No biggie. You're here now. What's
> the big whoop?

He tries to hand Erica a copy of his script.

                    CHAD
          Read this, baby. Please.

                    ERICA
          No! I don't feel like reading. It's
          two o'clock in the morning.

                    CHAD
          C'mon, baby. I need you. I have no
          one else to read my work -- and
          writing with no readers is like
          talking with no listeners. Besides,
          no one's opinion means more to me
          than yours.

                    ERICA
          I'm glad you think so highly of me,
          but what about what I need?

Chad stands confused.

                    ERICA
          Don't look like you don't know what
          I'm talking about. We've only been
          through this a million times.

                    CHAD
          I know it's late, but I was working
          on my script.

Erica leaves him standing with his pleading arms as she heads
for the living room.

## INT. ERICA'S LIVING ROOM - WEE HOURS

Erica pops on a night lamp and sits on her sofa with one leg
folded under her. The other dangles. Chad enters the living
room and stands in front of her.

                    ERICA
          Writing your script is not my beef.
          I needed you today.

                    CHAD
               (sitting)
          I'm sorry?

                    ERICA
          You said you'd be back around noon,
          but you did a no-show, a no-call,
          and you pop up here two in the
          morning -- and you have the nerve
          to ask me to read some script.

He places his hand on her leg. She pushes his hand away.

                    CHAD
          I just thought I was onto something
          good. I got excited, and I wanted
          to share it with you. I'm sorry,
          baby.

She reaches for his hand and places it back on her leg.

                    ERICA
          I'm sorry too. I don't want to
          discourage your writing, but I need
          you to take better care. Call me.
          Check on me -- see if I'm okay. I
          demand that from you. And not to be
          in control, but because I need it.

                    CHAD
          I'll do better, baby. I just get so
          hyped up when I think I'm on to
          something. I can't wait to get it
          to you, so you can read it, and
          give me your opinion. I guess I
          never stop to think what you need.
          I figure a bright and strong girl
          like you knows how to be okay.

                    ERICA
          Why -- because I don't sweat and
          break into hysterics?

                    CHAD
          I don't know. I guess.

                    ERICA
          Just because I'm a certain amount
          of smart, or a certain amount of
          reasonable, or even a certain
          amount of strong -- doesn't mean
          that everything is all right. At
          the end of the day I'm still a
          woman, and I need to be loved.

                    CHAD
          What do you want me to do?

                    ERICA
          I'm thirty, baby. I want to get
          married and have another child
          before it's too late.

                    CHAD
               (whatever)
          Okay, let's do it.

                    ERICA
          Don't play with my patience. Today
          has been crazy enough. I don't need
          anymore b.s.

Erica gets up and goes to her PC. She's about to log-on, but
shoves the keyboard to the floor instead. She's very
emotional. Chad runs over.

                    CHAD
               (concerned)
          Hey -- What's going on?

                    ERICA
          Lisa's dead!

                    CHAD
               (unbelievable)
          What...?

                    ERICA
          Yeah! Some 23 year old, preying on
          teenage girls -- the culprit of
          romantic jealousy, which caused
          another girl to stab Lisa to death.
          And she was pregnant, Chad!

                    CHAD
               (stunned)
          Wow... that's some crazy... heavy
          shit.

                    ERICA
          Lisa was so young. And her parents
          are so lost. Fighting too much to
          even notice she was pregnant.
               (clouded)
          The dynamic of a man and a woman
          not being able to get along is all
          to real. I'm not sure men and women
          really ought to be.

                    CHAD
          C'mon, baby.

                    ERICA
        Chad, I think we should call it
        quits. It's been two years, and I
        still don't know enough about you.

                    CHAD (V.O.)
        I know that Erica is right, but I
        don't want to lose her. It aches my
        heart to think it might be over
        between us.

                    ERICA
        You should go now.

                    CHAD
        Baby, there's a lot on your plate.

                    ERICA
        You're right. That's why you should
        go. My emotional bank is depleted.


                    CHAD
        I'll give you some room to breath,
        and hopefully you'll reconsider.

                    ERICA
             (sticking to her guns)
        Chad, we've been through this
        before -- I know how this goes.
        You're gunnuh get on your game for
        the next few months, and once you
        think things are patched up, you're
        gunnuh start slipping again. And in
        five months we'll be right here
        again! I can't do it. This is
        officially a break-up.

Chad's face droops with fear and pain.

                    CHAD (V.O.)
        I know she means it. And it hurts.
        She's right -- there's just too
        much going on in my life that she
        doesn't know about, and it would be
        unfair to keep her hanging on.

Erica reads the confusion in his face. She cuddles closely.

                    ERICA
        I love you with all my heart, but
        I've given all that I can.
                    (MORE)

                    ERICA (cont'd)
          I don't feel like I'm growing in
          this relationship anymore. So if
          you love me, let me go.

                    CHAD
               (worried)
          Is there someone else?

                    ERICA
          There's no one else. I just feel,
          in my heart, that taking some time
          off is the right thing to do. This
          relationship hasn't necessarily
          grown sweeter with time -- we just
          came this far because I chose to
          love you -- even when I felt in my
          heart that things weren't right.
          But no more.

He pecks her lips. She accepts. He pecks again. Her eyes
close. He glides his tongue in her mouth. She likes it, but
she pulls away.

Erica lies on her stomach across the couch. She closes her
eyes.

                    ERICA
          Please don't make this any harder
          than it already is.

Chad is lost momentarily. He gets up and walks to the desk.
He jots down his thoughts. Erica looks up.

                    ERICA
               (soft)
          Are you okay?

                    CHAD
          Hold on.

                    ERICA
          What are you doing?

                    CHAD
          Nothing.

                    ERICA
               (sitting up)
          What are you writing?

Chad holds up the paper. Erica begins reading it. She jumps
off the couch and tries to snatch the paper.

Chad struggles to stuff the paper in his pocket. Erica tries
to wrestle it free from his hand. He pulls away, retaining
the paper.

>                    ERICA
>          You wrote my words again!? Give it
>          to me, Chad.

>                    CHAD
>          It's my words. I wrote them.

>                    ERICA
>          But, I spoke them. Give it to me,
>          Chad.

>                    CHAD
>          No. It's not plagiarism. I didn't
>          just steal your words. It was our
>          conversation, so I have the right
>          to write it down.

>                    ERICA
>          No you don't! Those are my words,
>          and I don't want them in one of
>          your scripts. You want to use my
>          words to create some character for
>          a great story so you can blow up
>          and forget about me -- I don't
>          think so! Give me my words!

She attacks him with punches, tugs, and pushes. Chad takes
one on the chin.

She drags him to the foyer. Chad gently wrestles to control
her. He grips her forearms.

Erica is in utter panic! She bats her eyes with sheer
disappointment.

>                    ERICA
>          You don't have any respect for me
>          and what I feel.

>                    CHAD
>          What is the big deal? Why are you
>          losing it -- what is wrong with
>          you?

>                    ERICA
>          Get off of me! Let go of my arms!

She struggles to break free, but Chad maintains control
momentarily.

Finally, she yanks away! Her respirations are rapid and
heavy. Her eyes shine with a glossy emergence.

>           ERICA
> I asked you not to do that, but you
> did it anyway.
>      (she sobs)
> Didn't I ask you not to do it?

>           CHAD
> Yeah, but, Erica, c'mon.

>           ERICA
> It's not c'mon, Chad. Give me my
> words.

She reaches for the paper, but Chad pulls away. She wipes her
tears with her hand, then She wipes mucus from the tip of her
nose. She points to the door.

Chad shakes his fist at the ceiling.

>           CHAD
> What is it with this sniveling
> shit!

>           ERICA
> Get out, Chad!

>           CHAD
> Why do I have to leave?

>           ERICA
> Because I don't think you care
> about me. And I'm not a sniveling
> shit.

>           CHAD
> I'm not saying you're a sniveling
> shit. I'm saying what you're doing,
> is sniveling shit.

>           ERICA
> You don't care about the things I
> ask you not to do.

>           CHAD
> Erica, I ca-

                    ERICA
          All you care about is my words! If
          you were as wrapped up in me as you
          were with my words we'd be married
          already.

His cheeks puff with air. He exhales slowly as he drops his
back against the wall.

                    CHAD
          Baby, you're the one who's inspired
          me to write.

                    ERICA
          I'm glad to be a positive force in
          your life. When are you going to be
          one in mine?

                    CHAD
          You gave me this drive, don't take
          it away.

                    ERICA
          I don't want to take away your
          drive to write. But, I do want to
          be able to share my feelings with
          you, without the fear of being
          recorded in some way.

                    CHAD
          You can do that. You really can.

                    ERICA
              (shaking her head)
          No. I can't!

Chad stretches his face to within an inch of Erica's. She
pushes him by the shoulder.

                    ERICA
          Back up, Chad.

                    CHAD
          Why can't you share your feelings
          with me?

                    ERICA
              (burst into angry tears)
          Because! I can pour my heart out to
          you, but before you soothe me you
          have to write my words down -- how
          do you think that makes me feel?
              (MORE)

                        ERICA (cont'd)
          You notice my words, but you don't
          notice me.

Chad looks on with a long face. He attempts to console her
with a hug -- she wants to accept, but fights him off
instead.

                        ERICA
          Don't touch me.

                        CHAD
          I'm sorry that the words you speak
          inspire me in such a way that I
          feel I must write them down. To me
          you're so smart. So witty. Half of
          what you say I forget in my haste
          to remember. You're like a walking
          library, and I try to absorb as
          much from you as I can. The words
          you speak come alive. The things I
          understand from you make a great
          story. Perspectives that come from
          a brilliant mind. Emotions that
          flow from a mighty heart.

Erica stands at the door, her face sad and streaming with
tears. Her chest still jumping with heavy respirations. Yet,
Chad's able to calm her slightly as she wipes away some more
tears.

                        ERICA
          That was sweet. I truly appreciate
          it, but I'm more than words.

                        CHAD
          I know, Baby.

                        ERICA
          Well, when are you going to act
          like it!?

                        CHAD
          Baby, I-

                        ERICA
          I sit here and tell you all that's
          on my mind and in my heart -- all
          my fears and discomforts. I tell
          you Lisa is dead! And you do
          nothing to fix it. You just wait
          for me to shut up so you can write
          down my words. I'm more than words,
          Chad. I'm more than words!

                    CHAD
          Yes, you are.

                    ERICA
          I want you to go now.

                    CHAD
          Baby, I had no idea it actually
          bothered you this much. I'm sorry --
          I love you so much, baby.

                    ERICA
          When are you going to give to me
          what I give to you?

                    CHAD
          What do you need from me?

                    ERICA
          When can I get the attention my
          words get? When can I get the
          respect my words get?
               (she sobs)
          When can I get the love my words
          get? You're hurting me Chad -- bad.
          Am I just your muse, or do you
          really love me?

Chad's eyes shine with pain as he sees that she is truly
hurting.

                    CHAD
          Baby...

                    ERICA
          No more talk, Chad. Not now. Let it
          process.  Then, show me. I dare
          you.

Chad throws his hands against the wall in an emotional fit.

                    CHAD
          Okay! I'm done writing. Bright and
          early Monday morning I'll start
          looking for a job. A regular nine
          to five. No more wasting my time
          with writing.

                    ERICA
          That's up to you. You can run from
          this if you'd like, because it's
          only running from commitment. But
          You're a writer, Chad.
               (MORE)

                    ERICA (cont'd)
          Run from that, and you're running
          from yourself.

                    CHAD
          What do you mean -- I'm committed
          to you!

                    ERICA
                (fed with his bullshit!)
          Who do you share your resources
          with!? Where do you sleep at
          night!? You've slept here maybe
          four times in two years. You say
          this is a relationship, Chad, but I
          feel so alone.

Chad's discouraged and lost for words -- he knows she's
right.

                    CHAD
          Get some rest. I'll call you
          tomorrow.

                    ERICA
          Don't bother, because I'm not sure
          I'm talking to you.

                    CHAD
          What -- I can't call you anymore?

                    ERICA
          Space is the key word, Chad. A <u>lot</u>
          of it.

                    CHAD
          Eric-

                    ERICA
          Bye, Chad!

She opens the door. He tosses his script on the floor. She
shoves him out and SLAMS the door behind him.


## INT. ONE WEST - WEE HOURS

Chad is the last customer. He looks defeated. He throws his
head back and downs his final shot. He BANGS his empty glass
on the counter.

                    CHAD
          Arrghhh!

Lights are turning off in the BG. Chad tosses some bills on the counter. Charlie approaches.

                    CHARLIE
               (curious)
          This isn't like you, Chad.

                    CHAD
               (drunk)
          How do I tell her I have a two year
          old boy, Charlie?

                    CHARLIE
          I don't have that answer.

                    CHAD
          I have a certain allegiance and
          loyalties to Lana, but my heart is
          with Erica.

                    CHARLIE
          Let me tell you what my daddy
          always told me.

                    CHAD
          What's that, Charlie?

                    CHARLIE
          "A man's role in the family is
          limited. Especially if he plays the
          field."

                    CHAD
          Even if I tell Erica the truth, it
          won't fix the damage. I don't know
          how I will live without her. Who
          will she love next?

                    CHARLIE
          Hey, man. Keep your wits about you.
          Don't start thinking crazy. You got
          Lana and the kids to look after. If
          this Erica is any kind of woman,
          she'll understand.

                    CHAD
          Yeah. I'm sure she will. I just
          don't understand, Charlie.

He squirms from his stool. His eyes spacey -- like he may do
anything. He staggers for the door. Just before he exits-

>               CHARLIE
>          Hey!

Chad turns.

>               CHARLIE
>            (strong)
>          It's a tough world out there.
>          Families need fathers. That strong
>          figure to nourish them against the
>          odds.

Chad stares a beat. The words appears to have sunk in. Chad
staggers out the door.


**EXT. CHAD'S HOUSE - BED ROOM - WEE HOURS**

Lana is in the bed asleep, but doesn't look peaceful. Chad Jr
is nestled under her.

Chad enters. He quietly grab some blankets from the closet
and makes a pallet on the floor, then stretches out.


**INT. ERICA'S BEDROOM - WEE HOURS**

Erica sits up in bed clutching a small picture frame to her
chest. Her lamp glowing against her face. She kisses the
photo, then places it on her night stand. The picture is
Chad.

A tear sneaks from the corner of her eye. She climbs out of
bed and walks to her trash basket where she retrieves Chad's
script.

She wipes it clean with her hand. She reads the title,
"American Tragedy." She opens the script and begins reading.


**INT. CHAD'S KITCHEN - DAWN**

The house is quiet. Everyone's still asleep except Chad. He's
at the fusion station brewing a mug of tea. He's suited in
all black.


**INT. ERICA'S APARTMENT - MORNING**

Erica opens the door, and it's Chad. He's holding a single
red rose, a Heresy's bar, and a card.

Erica steps aside with a smile. She's really glad to see him.
He hands her the gifts as he enter.

                    ERICA
          Thank you.

They hug a beat.

                    CHAD
               (emotional, but strong)
          I appreciate you being able to love
          me no matter what I do. I thank you
          for continuing to pull me out the
          swamp.

                    ERICA
          It's the natural thing to do when
          you love someone.

                    CHAD
          McDonald's, Shoprite, or whatever.
          It excites my heart to know that
          that's enough for you. But, baby,
          it's not enough for me. I don't
          have the credentials or the
          experience to tackle this corporate
          world. I've already fumbled eight
          years of my life, and I don't have
          a real pension to work toward.

                    ERICA
          I understand. I truly do, but you
          need a job, at least for the
          survival of day-to-day living.

                    CHAD
          Applying for a job is close to
          useless -- you got pre-employment
          agencies doing criminal background
          investigations, screening my files
          and exposing my life. What
          worthwhile company's going to hire
          me after discovering I'm a
          convicted felon?

                    ERICA
               (emotional)
          Baby, I know being an ex-con with
          no job is real for you. And I don't
          mean to buck your philosophy, but
          that's only the situation you're
          in. It's not who you are.

                    CHAD
          It seems like a descent guy with a
          clean mind should be able to make a
          fair living.

A tear drops from each of his eyes. The sight of his pain
weakens Erica. She latches onto his hands.

                    ERICA
          I understand you. But think about
          it from a business standpoint.
          Here's a guy who easily qualifies
          for a position -- there's the
          clarity. But, he has a criminal
          record -- there's the vagueness.
          Accept that, but don't let it
          control you.

                    CHAD
               (he mans up)
          All I have left, that I believe in,
          is my writing. And that's how I'm
          going to graduate in this world.
          That's how I'm going to survive the
          onslaught.

                    ERICA
          Baby, you sound so courageous.
               (beat)
          I read your story, and it was done
          so well. It seems autobiographical.
          I'm proud of you. And I'm so sorry,
          baby. I shouldn't have pushed you
          like that. I shouldn't have done
          that to you. I feel so uptight and
          freaked out by it all. I had no
          idea you thought it through so
          deeply. I don't want you to quit
          writing. It's just, I feel like
          such a tremendous loser, and I'm so
          afraid you're going to blow-up and
          leave me behind.

                    CHAD
          Never.

                    ERICA
          I'm sorry I've been such a source
          of confusion for you. I'm trying
          with all my might to remember that
          there is value in trials and
          tribulations, but I just don't have
          much figured out.

He holds her.

                    CHAD
          It's okay.

Erica's eyes are sad, as if she's hiding a burden she can no
longer keep inside.

                    ERICA
          I haven't been totally honest about
          everything that I'm really going
          through, baby. I took so much out
          on you, which you really didn't
          deserve. Excuse my French, but my
          shit is so not together

                    CHAD
          Shh, shh, shh... it's okay.
               (as he rocks her in his
                arms)

                    ERICA
          It's not okay. Baby, my career is
          in jeopardy, which puts my life in
          jeopardy. If I fail, who's gunnuh
          take care of Bria? Tom is such a
          jerk.

                    CHAD
               (confused)
          What are you talking about?

                    ERICA
               (sad; confused)
          I never graduated with my masters.
          When I was with Tom, I took time
          off, at his request, to care for
          Bria so he could finish his
          Master's. Once he finished, we were
          supposed to switch roles so I could
          finish. It never happened. Now this
          jerk is doing like 70 a year. My
          job offered me a promotion that
          would put me at 65, but I can't
          accept it.

                    CHAD
          Why?

                    ERICA
          Background checks -- academic
          investigation.
               (MORE)

                    ERICA (cont'd)
And if they find out, not only will
they fire me, but they can sue my
ass. Then with my great luck,
you'll become a famous writer and
forget all about me. Why can't I
find a man to truly love me back?
Why do some hearts have it easy and
some don't?

Chad understands, and he is sympathetic to her plight as he
pulls her close and consoles her.

She stares him in the face. He looks like he wants to talk,
and that guilt is getting the best of him.

                    CHAD (V.O.)
I wish my life was less confusing.
I would really like to make her
life happy.

Erica senses something wrong in her heart. She puts her head
on his chest.

                    ERICA
You seem to manage the absolute
worst of me so well, baby. Thank
you. I just don't know what I will
do if this doesn't work out -- I
mean, if this isn't real what is?

She squeezes him tighter and begins to cry. Then she looks
upward, straight into his eyes.

                    ERICA
Now you know everything about me.
Is there anything I need to know
about you? What's keeping you from
choosing this?

He takes a deep breath but says nothing. However, his eyes
are telling their own story.  She wipes her tears then his.

                    ERICA
Baby, life is about choices. The
ones you make and the ones you
don't. So, what is it? You settled
in with your daughters mother --
another baby -- one on the way --
what? I feel like you're committed
to someone else. I mean, I love the
love we share, but I want the
relationship too. If you can't do
it, then let me go. Please.

                    CHAD (V.O.)
          I couldn't believe the strength of
          her intuition. I wanted to be
          honest so badly -- but I didn't
          want to hurt her anymore. And I
          didn't want to risk losing her
          beyond reconciliation. I wish I
          could have been a better man to her
          -- a better person in general. I'm
          defeated with trying to hold on to
          her through lies and deceit.

They stare each other in the eyes for a passionate beat.
Tears stream both of their faces. They lock lips and kiss
passionately -- They both know it's probably their last kiss.


MONTAGE

Young Hearts Run Free, by Candi Stanton carries montage.


**EXT. CHURCH - DAY**

The parking lot is full. A  white Hurst and two white limos
are parked out front, along the curbside.

Plenty of teens who couldn't fit inside are spilling out onto
the church steps.


**INT. CHURCH - DAY**

High school students fill the pews. They sit shoulder to
shoulder, and standers fill the outside aisles -- all their
eyes dripping tears.

Erica is in the second row, beside Ms. Lucy and Drake.
They're all sad, but Erica is devastated.

Stephanie is in the front pew, sitting beside a deeply
saddened Rosina. Both their faces wet from uncontrollable
tears, but Rosina is crying the pain only a mother could cry
for a lost child.

Beside Rosina is an empty seat -- Woodrow isn't there.


**EXT. URBAN STREET - IN FRONT OF KENNETH'S HOUSE - DAY**

Kenneth is being dragged to a squad car. He's shoved into
the back seat.

**EXT. PARK - ON JUNGLE GYM - DAY**

Yvonne and her home girls are downing beers, and drinking themselves into a stupor. They all appear worried and regretful.

Suddenly, Police rush up and spring from squad cars with their guns drawn. The girls are terrified -- they throw their hands to the air, dropping their beer bottles, which EXPLODE against the asphalt.


**EXT. A LOCAL BRIDGE - NIGHT**

Security lamps from dockside buildings glow against the river water.

Chad stands on the bridge overlooking the river. He doesn't look as if he wants to jump, though -- it seems the setting presents a soothing quality for him.

Farther down the catwalk of the bridge Erica is walks away. Her steps really dragging. WE MOVE IN CLOSER -- films of tears streak her cheeks.

Her face contorts to fight back the pain -- her eyes blink back and forth, to fight the tears.

                                        MONTAGE ENDS


**INT. DR. LEVIN'S - NEXT DAY**

Chad is back on the couch. Dr. Levin sits beside him.

                    DR. LEVIN
            Now tell me about your dad. What
            was he like?

                    CHAD
        Well--


**FLASHBACK -- CHRISTMAS DAY - 1977**


**INT. LIVING ROOM - MORNING**

Lights twinkle from the decorated tree. Opened gifts are scattered about. 135 pounds in weights sit on the floor. We hear a DOOR BELL RING.

Two TEENAGE BOYS compete to open the door. They yank it open together.

Standing outside the door is **BIG GARY**, Chad's dad. A man tall in height with a goatee. Seven-year-old Chad is by his side. They enter.

Big Gary has a gentle voice and feminine demeanor -- almost homosexual-like to some.

                    BIG GARY
          Hey boys. Where's Aunt Mary?

                    TEEN #1
          Hi, Big Gary. She's washing in the
          basement. What's up Chad.

Chad runs to the weights. He tries lifting.

                    BIG GARY
          Don't touch those weights. You'll
          get a hernia.

                    TEEN #1
               (snickering)
          Can you lift that, Big Gary?

Big Gary squats, somewhat feminine. He attempts to lift the weights, but he can't budge them.

                    BIG GARY
          Oh, no. Too much for me.

Teen #1 quickly runs over and lifts the weights to outdo Big Gary. Big Gary could care less, but Chad is ashamed.

                    BIG GARY
               (lightly winded)
          That's for you younger guys.

Big Gary slaps Chad five and leaves out. After teen #1 closes the door behind him, he and teen #2 snicker at Chad.

                    TEEN #2
          When you grow up, you goin' be gay
          just like your father.

The teens giggle wildly. Chad is hurt and ashamed.

**BACK TO SCENE**

Chad lies across the couch in emotional pain as DR. Levin takes notes.

>                    DR. LEVIN
>          How did he and your mother get
>          along?

>                    CHAD
>          I'll tell you.

**FLASHBACK - 1977**

**INT. CANDY STORE - DAY**

Chad is pleading with his dad to buy him candy and a soda pop when a female patron rudely approaches.

>                    FEMALE PATRON
>                    (gossipy)
>          Gary, let me tell you, you did
>          right by leaving his mother, cause
>          I heard she sleeping with two or
>          three different men.

Chad stares on with disappointment.

**INT. BEAUTY PARLOR - DAY**

Chad is at the receptionist desk with his mom, an attractive, sassy woman.

>                    RECEPTIONIST
>                    (shocked; to Chad's mom)
>          I heard he went the other way, and
>          he's sleeping around with Bobby
>          Jackson, and some other man.

Chad looks on, deeply saddened.

**INT. MINI MART - 1977 - DAY**

Chad is shopping with his dad when they unexpectedly run into his mom. She and his dad immediately exchange fiery stares.

>                    CHAD'S MOM
>          Why didn't you bring him to me this
>          past weekend!?

>           BIG GARY
> What do you care. I hear you're
> busy sleeping with every man in
> town.

>           CHAD'S MOM
>      (right back at ya!)
> And I hear, I ain't the only one.
> Your story is making it's
> conversational rounds, too!

Big Gary yanks Chad by the hand and angrily walks off,
leaving his cart behind. Chad sadly looks over his shoulder
and waves good-bye to his mother.


**BACK TO SCENE**

Chad lies on the couch staring blankly at the ceiling.

>           DR. LEVIN
> It seems your childhood was
> challenging. One could guess you
> went thugging around, gun-slinging,
> drug dealing, and woman hopping to
> distinguish your identity from that
> of your father's. You needed to be
> sure you didn't have his
> tendencies.

>           CHAD
> Could that be valid, Doc?

>           DR. LEVIN
> Sure. That, and your size issues
> could have plenty to do with it?

>           CHAD
>      (confused)
> How does the two fit into me being
> a loser?

>           DR. LEVIN
> You feared not being able to
> satisfy a woman's wild sexual
> cravings, due to your size
> insecurities, yet, you had to find
> a legitimate reason to take pride
> in your penis. Thus, you chalked up
> women like they were points on a
> scoring card.

                    CHAD
               (discouraged)
          I'm just a fucked up individual.

                    DR. LEVIN
          You have serious obstructing
          issues. Childhood marks of shame
          that interfere with your conduct
          toward women, and life in general.

                    CHAD
               (regretful)
          I had to let Erica go yesterday,
          Doc -- the most amazing woman that
          I've ever met. The woman that loves
          me just the right way. The woman I
          enjoy most and communicate with
          best. The true, perfect fit for me.

                    DR. LEVIN
          So Why did you let her go?

Emotional beat for Chad.

                    CHAD
          Because I love her, Doc. That's
          why.

                    DR. LEVIN
          I guess you explained Lana, Chad
          Jr., and your mistress with the new
          expectancy?

As Chad lie on the couch, his head wiggles as if he's trying
to shake off the painful truth, and his expression changes.
He blinks gently.

                    CHAD
          You don't share pain like that. You
          keep that truth -- it would be
          cruel to disclose it. You just say,
          "I'm sorry. It's me, not you." And
          you walk. You just walk, Doc.

Chad wipes his eyes. He sits up. He takes a deep breath, then
lies back down. The doctor stares for a curious beat.

                    DR. LEVIN
          Do care about Lana's heart, and
          what she feels?

                    CHAD
          I want the weight of the world off
          my chest, Doc, but at this point,
          being honest is only a selfish step
          toward healing my own pain. I need
          to consider the pain my harsh
          truths will inflict upon the hearts
          of others. I'm at the end of my
          rope. There's just no solution.

                    DR. LEVIN
          In the game of life, no one gets
          out alive, but you should never
          give up.

                    CHAD
          I feel like it's all over, and I'm
          only 29.

                    DR. LEVIN
          Love is a fire that can burn your
          heart with warmth, or it can burn
          it with fury. All depends on what
          you fuel it with.
               (beat)
          My wife and I have been married and
          in love for thirty-five years. We
          fuel our love with reliability,
          honesty, romance, and commitment.
          It burns are hearts with warmth.

                    CHAD
          That's a great thing to say, Doc.
          But with a problem like mine, it's
          a difficult thing do. I'm no good
          for any woman, Doc. I'm a virus to
          women, which makes my own life no
          worthless.


**EXT. URBAN STREETS - MCDONALD'S - DAY**

Chad approaches the fast food establishment. There's a shrine
in memory of Lisa.

Chad's all choked up. He pats his pockets and draws a pen. He
signs the poster-board. He steps back and sadly looks on.

A van pulls up to the curbside. It's plastered with "Great
Care for Girls" along the side panels. Stephanie gets out the
passenger door.

She's carries flowers and a rolled up poster. She places the flowers with all the rest. She unrolls the poster-sized picture of her and Stephanie, and she tapes it on the McDonald's building.

Stephanie burst into distress and runs back to the van.

Chad stares, wishing he could help. His eyes blink in an effort to fight his tears. He walks away after one last glance at the shrine.

**INT. ONE WEST - DAY**

Chad is alone at a table. His head down. Charlie approaches.

> CHARLIE
> Let me give you some advice, young
> man. Get over this. Grief pollutes
> the heart. Polluted hearts crush
> the soul. And a crushed soul is
> unpredictable.

MONTAGE

**EXT. URBAN STREETS - ALLEY - DAY**

It's a narrow pathway between two buildings, which leads from a back parking lot to the main avenue.

Bums use the alley to discard bottles, and relieve their bladders.

Woodrow, still suited in his army apparel, is spraddled across a litter of empty bottles and broken glass. The ground where he lay and the crotch of his pants are stained with urine.

His eyes are rolled behind his head. His flagon of vodka still clutched in his hand, while Side Show, by Blue Magic CROONS from his portable radio, which lies beside him.

Police, ambulance, and the medical examiner pull into the back parking lot. They enter the alley.

Onlookers are viewing into the alley from the main avenue.

The medical examiner checks his vital signs. He's dead. They cover him with a white sheet.

**INT. BANKS APARTMENT - BATHROOM - DAY**

We TRACK through and notice that the window sill, the walls, and the tub are all plagued with indoor mildew.

The leaky faucet DRIP-DRIPS into the rust-stained sink.

The Medicine cabinet is swung open. Various prescription bottles lay carelessly, few pills are scattered about.

We angle downward to the floor and just as we feared, we witness Rosina, sprawled out. Her eyes open wide, and her mouth gaping. She's gone.

MONTAGE ENDS

**INT. DINNER - EVENING**

Shelly and Dr. Levin are seated. A **WAITER** approaches and places menus.

                    WAITER
          Good evening. Can get you something
          to drink?

                    SHELLY
          Yes. Two Martinis. But we're
          waiting for a third party before we
          order dinner.

                    WAITER
          That's fine. I'll be right back
          with your drinks.

The waiter leaves.

                    SHELLY
               (peering)
          He's never late. I reminded him of
          the time, date, and location
          earlier today. He said he'd be
          here.

                    DR. LEVIN
          I am really looking forward to
          finally meeting this writer. His
          story reminds me so much of this
          new client of mine.

                    SHELLY
          Chad's story is so realistic.

DR. LEVIN
(surprised)
Did you say "Chad?"

SHELLY
Yeah -- why?

DR. LEVIN
I thought the author's name was
William Wilson?

SHELLY
That's his pseudonym. His name is
Chad Miller.

DR. LEVIN
What!?

**FLASHBACK**

**EXT. PARKING LOT - DAY**

Sean keeps a wary gaze on Chad, this furious stranger to him,
as he stoops to retrieve his satchel and personals.

Sean can see Chad's fury mounting as he gathers his things.

CHAD
You piece of shit!

SEAN
(his voice breaks)
Now there's a contradiction. You
say don't ever disrespect you. An-
and you call me a "Piece of shit."

**BACK TO SCENE**

DR. LEVIN
Oh no. This is too paradoxical.

SHELLY
What?

DR. LEVIN
Chad Miller. He's my client. We've
met. Under the unlikeliest of
circumstances. I cant believe he's
the writer!
(holding the script)
(MORE)

                    DR. LEVIN (cont'd)
          This isn't some random story. This
          guy is on edge.

                    SHELLY
                    (worried)
          What are you saying.

                    DR. LEVIN
                    (disappointed)
          I may have failed him. I wouldn't
          be surprised if he doesn't show up
          tonight. Or any other night.

                    SHELLY
                    (grabs cellular)
          You're scaring me, Sean.


**EXT. URBAN GAS STATION - EVENING**

A teen pulls up to the air pump with his car stereo BLASTING
Don't Let Me Be misunderstood, by Santa Esmeralda.

As the teen gets out to fill his tire with air he bobs his
head to the lyrics, "I'm just a soul who's intentions are
good, oh Lord, please don't let me be misunderstood."

Then the teen blows a kiss to the giddy girl in the passenger
seat of his ride as he walks to the men's room. The door
already ajar. He pushes it completely open. HUH!

The walls are spattered red. Legs are outstretched from the
commode -- arms dangle lifelessly -- a bloodstained pistol
lie on the floor.

Finally, we see the apparent suicide victim but we can't make
out who it is because the man's bloodstained face is slumped
into his chest.


**EXT. OPEN ROAD - ON AMBULANCE - REAR - EVENING**

Its FLASHERS going and the sirens WAILING. We follow the
ambulance down the lonely road until it becomes a dot in our
vision.


**INT. CHAD'S LIVING ROOM - EVENING**

Lana hangs up the phone. She's ecstatic. She writes on tablet
paper,then plasters the sticky on the sub-zero.

CLOSE ON STICKY

It reads: *Your agent called. You did it! A six-figure deal. So proud of you. She's waiting for you at diner. Hope you showed up. Oh, we're expecting again:-).*

## EXT. ERICA'S LIVING ROOM - NIGHT

Erica sits on the love seat rocking Bria in her arms -- she's rocking her with purpose, like Bria is the one thing that's keeping it all together for her.

## INT. CHAD'S LIVING ROOM - NIGHT

Lana's peeking out the window. No signs of Chad, and She is depressed. Then, the phone RINGS. Lana scurries for the cordless. Don't Leave Me This Way,by Thelma Houston CROONS in BG.

The kids look on with hope that it's dad. Beat. Lana looks different, and she goes off to use the phone in private.

Her face in hope and pain -- almost like a prayer. Then, her face takes another change. An emotional change. The phone drops. She breaks down.

> ERICA (V.O.)
> Chad was struggling with emotional
> and morale commitment between Lana
> and I. In the process of breaking
> our hearts, Chad broke his own
> heart.
> (beat)
> He was tortured internally. A
> divided soul. Driven by angels in
> one instance, and driven by the
> devil in another. Lana was his
> commitment that lacked romance, and
> I was his romance that lacked
> commitment. He was so confused, and
> ended up a broken man.

## EXT. ABORTION CLINIC - DAY

Janice warily eases through a hostile crowd of ABORTION ACTIVIST. Her face drooping with depression. She weaves through their goal-line stance and makes it safely to the door.

>                    ERICA (V.O.)
>          She was another of Chad's victims
>          whom cared much about him. I think
>          he knew it and appreciated her, but
>          he was just in too deep to make any
>          of us really feel appreciated back.

## INT. ERICA'S LIVING ROOM - DAY

Erica's dressed in black. She wipes her tears and places an
obituary on the coffee table.

CLOSE ON OBITUARY

To our horror, Chad's friendly smile taking up the picture
box.

## EXT. CEMETERY - RAINING - DAY

A motorcade of limousines drive slowly through the burial
site. Water sprays from the tires.

Funeral Procession in progress. Speaker gives final words.
Loved ones toss roses onto casket.

People hug and depart toward their vehicles. Lana and her
children remain standing, alone.

Finally, Lana turns to leave. Wipes her eyes. She carries
Chad Jr in her arms. The three girls along side her. They're
all emotionally drained. A heart-wrenching sight.

Lana is Barely able to keep her balance through a fit of pain
as her daughter Joy has to catch Chad Jr from her arms While
Sabrina and Diana struggle to keep Lana on her feet.

>                    ERICA (V.O.)
>          Knowing neither I, nor Lana would
>          applaud him for his horrible truth,
>          Chad stubbornly clung to his dirty
>          secrets. And just as most men, Chad
>          was unable to nurse his own inner
>          wounds. Rather than live with the
>          guilt, he chose to abandon life.
>          Took the easy way out. Selfishness
>          on the last level. What a poor
>          choice.

**EXT. SHORELINE - EVENING**

Clouds roll across a cherry sky. Waves CRASH rock-bed.
Somewhere out there a buoy DONGS.

Gulls GAWK and take flight. A piece of litter whirls around,
then blows away.

>                    CHAD (V.O.)
>          (regretful)
>     All my distress was of my own
>     creation, and I was past cure. I
>     couldn't maintain a simple domestic
>     life for a family that loved me. So
>     busy running from who I was afraid
>     to become, I chased myself into not
>     knowing who I was anymore. Life
>     began to make me cooky.
>          (beat)
>     Have you ever dreamed of a place
>     where life is not a struggle, but a
>     lasting delight? I read that
>     somewhere and it made me think.
>          (beat)
>     Here's a quote from Thomas Wolfe
>     in, God's Lonely Man.
>          (beat)
>     "The whole conviction of my life
>     now rest upon the belief that
>     loneliness, far from being a rare
>     and curious phenomenon, is the
>     central and inevitable fact of
>     human existence."

                                        FADE OUT.

# GLOSSARY OF INDUSTRY TERMS

**INT.** - INTERIOR - SCENE INTRO that indicates a set representing an indoor scene.

**EXT.** - EXTERIOR - SCENE INTRO that indicates a set representing an outdoor scene.

**(V.O.)** - VOICE OVER - Off screen commentary, like narration, when a character's voice is heard over the action of a scene.

**(O.S.)** - OFF SCREEN - Dialogue of a character while the camera is on another subject.

**BEAT** - BREAK IN PROCEEDINGS - in a screenplay, this term is used to indicate a pause in a character's speech or action.

**MONTAGE** - A scene heading which indicates a rapid succession of shots.

**P.O.V. or POV** - (Point of view) - Camera position that views a scene from a particular viewpoint, or views a scene from the viewpoint of a particular character.

**CLOSE ON or CLOSEUP** - Camera position which indicates a close shot of a particular character or thing.

**PULL BACK** - When the camera zooms out to give the audience a broader view.

**BACKGROUND** - **(b.g.)** - Secondary sound, talk, or action that lends to a particular scene. EX: At a party the camera concentrates on one character, but common party noises are heard in the background (b.g.).

**FLASHBACK** - a retro scene that gives history to a character or several characters lives.

**BACK TO SCENE** - when the story returns to it original or initial scene after a flashback or a different P.O.V.

**TRACK THROUGH** - When the camera moves through a scene or setting, viewing it from various angles.

**SOTTO** - When a character speaks under their breath, to themselves.